Little Robin
Jo Priestley

Copyright © 2023 Jo Priestley

All rights reserved.

Dedication

If we are fortunate, we will experience many loves in our life – from the special bond of motherhood and family to romance – and we are all seeking that rare thing, unconditional love.

But such love often comes at a price and demands you set aside your own happiness and feelings for another's. This is the dilemma faced by the title character of my latest story.

My thanks to my dear friend Kelly for inspiring the title *Little Robin* and to Ann and Tracey for continuing to review and critique my writing. You constantly drive me forward to become a better writer.

Thank you again to Andrew for his support and excellent editing and to Megan for adapting the cover from artwork by Alana Jordan.

Last, but not least, I'd like to thank all my daughters for supporting their mother's journey as an author. I'm very grateful.

Chapter 1

Wednesday 25th September is a miserable day.

Perhaps not the worst of days but certainly a notably bad one. The weather turned so quickly, summer fled rather than floated away.

Five days ago, my makeshift bed would have felt warm at least but tonight the cold and dampness clings tightly to me. Even so I am so grateful for the little I have.

Dear Miss Wainwright, I think. I am nobody to her, yet she gave us a nook to sleep safely when I was desperately in need of shelter.

I'm fully clothed but shivering to the point of rattling teeth. I search the cupboard and find three torn sacks to replace the damp blanket. Their itchy roughness is the lesser of evils as I must find sleep to have strength for tomorrow. I can't risk becoming unwell.

As she cleared a corner of her windowless housekeeping store, Miss Wainwright had assured me I would be safe, that Mr Weatherall the nightwatchman would never venture into the sanctity of her private space. It was an unspoken rule he followed without question. Regardless, only she has a key, the key now on a hook by the door entrusted to one stranger by another.

Tomorrow morning, she will wait for Mr Weatherall to leave after his shift and knock three times on the door, pause and then knock a further three times. This is our code, a system we can use until she finds an alternative arrangement, she tells me. The rest of the endless day in the woodland is my own business, but I must return in the forty-five-minute gap between the end of the shift for the workers and the start of Mr Weatherall's nightshift. He always arrives precisely fifteen minutes before his start time.

"Do you understand, Renee?" she asked the first day, "I can't stress enough that you arrive no later than half-past six, no matter where you are or what you happen to be doing. I will be waiting for you."

"I understand, Miss Wainwright," I said obediently.

She stared at me a moment then nodded, satisfied the plan was in place. She handed me a white tea towel. I had already been imagining the food I knew was wrapped inside. I wanted to tear open the knot and devour every last scrap, but politeness prevailed.

"You must be famished," she said, her voice softening, her rheumy eyes kindness itself, "I will speak to Mr Mallerby, but I may not be able to secure a place in the factory or at the hall without references."

I wanted to cry, not because I might be unable to find work; I wanted to cry because of her compassion, her sympathy. I swallowed down the tears and looked down at my dress. I even owe the clothes on my back to this lady's benevolence.

I'd been sleeping for two nights in a semi-derelict storehouse at the rear of the factory before she found me. I can still recall the terror as her hand gently touched my shoulder and the shock of her voice, the first one I'd heard in three lonely days.

"What are you doing here, lass?" she asked, shawl clasped tightly between her bosom, salt and pepper hair pulled back into a bun. Wisping strands fell about her ears.

She grabbed my arm to help me when I tried to stand as I was unsteady from lack of food. She had strength and her hand was calloused, yet somehow her touch was gentle.

"I mean you no harm, I only want to help. There's no need to alarm yourself."

My best green dress was soiled—dusty and ripped slightly—torn on the nail of a ladder as I scaled the factory wall. Later, Miss Wainwright told me when she caught sight of me as she passed the door which had come ajar, I looked like a tatty ragdoll lying strewn on the floor. She said she had looked then looked again to be sure I was real.

As we stood together, she kept a firm hold of my arm as though I might flee at any moment.

"I'm sorry to trespass, I only took shelter last night and I'll be on my way now. Forgive me for taking the liberty," I said.

Her eyes roamed my face.

"Where are you from? You're not from round these parts with that accent."

What to tell her, how much to tell her, I had no idea, yet somehow, I knew from her expression and her manner I was in safe hands.

"The North Riding," I said, deciding on a modicum of truth.

Sighing, her eyebrows raised at the evasive answer. She pulled an old wooden stool from the corner, gesturing to me to sit down as she perched on the low windowsill. Glass was barely clinging to half the panes in the window.

"Now look, let's stop beating about the bush. If you've been staying in this midden miles from home, then you're clearly in some kind of trouble. If I were you, I'd get it all off your chest. If you tell me what's happened to you, I can see what I can do to help."

I was calmed; calmed and softly beaten into submission. But still shame wouldn't allow me to tell the whole truth.

"My family have disowned me, and I have nowhere to go," I told her flatly.

She wouldn't take kindly to me playing games. Though I was unable to maintain eye contact I had no intention of taking my Good Samaritan for a fool.

Her eyes never left my face as she considered my words. Finally, after I'd been left out to dry for too long, she leaned forward to offer her hand. I was taken aback but I took her hand and shook it once, feeling again that strange mix of roughness and tenderness in her palm.

"As you've been so honest, I won't press you further. I'm Miss Wainwright, the housekeeper of Mallerby Hall. I also clean Mr Mallerby's offices here at the clog factory. I'm the only person he trusts nowadays to be amongst his personal whatnots, home and away. What's your name?"

"Serena," I tell her, "Serena Wilton-Robbins."

I decided quickly not to lie but the name stopped her in her tracks. She sat a moment opening and closing her mouth. When she eventually got to her feet, she towered above me.

"Well, the way I see it there's generally only one reason a young girl is disowned by a posh family or any family for that matter. Tell me am I wrong?"

I stayed silent only confirming her suspicions. I was relieved not to have to explain my situation any further.

"I see," she said.

Those two words said so much. I didn't feel chastised or condemned but my face was on fire.

The corners of her mouth twitched.

"Right, well then, there's nothing else for it," she said, "As you've been cast adrift, I think I've no option but to throw you a rubber ring."

I'd no idea what she was talking about, but she clearly had a plan of some sort.

"Well, I do need some help at the hall there's no denying it, I'm fair rushed off my feet. So, if I'm to pass you off as my widowed cousin from up north we're going to have our work cut out. First off, it might not surprise you that no cousin of mine would be called Serena Wilton-Robbins."

I stared at her, and she let out a low chuckle.

"From now on you're to be known as Renee Robson. Yes, Renee Robson isn't too much of a stretch from your real name. I think it will do nicely."

My mouth hung loose at her precarious, even ludicrous plan.

But the alternative of trudging off alone into the cold world was enough to resign myself to it. Beggars, which is exactly what I have become, simply cannot be choosers.

Chapter 2

Three knocks at the door.

After a second or two I'm relieved to hear three more. I'd heard Mr Weatherall's footsteps too many times in the night. Each time, I was convinced I would cough or sneeze and be discovered by a bewildered and angry nightwatchman. I'd be out on the streets for a second time, but this time I'd be on my own for good. There can surely only be one angel in disguise. Only one Miss Wainwright in this world.

Scrambling to my feet I've no time to stretch my aching back as I don't wish to keep her waiting a second longer than necessary.

"Morning, Martha," I say as instructed, struggling to pull off the new dialect of my alter-ego, Renee. I'm turning a silk purse to a sow's ear, I think. To be accepted into another fold I must unpick and restuff myself with cotton and rags rather than fine silk and satin.

My instruction began immediately after Martha Wainwright decided on her course of action. I am her protégé and I sense she's enjoying the little break from routine. My mother would have called her a character.

"I'd like to repay you somehow," I tell her, "But I have little to offer."

"We'll have none of that talk if you don't mind, Renee. I need an extra pair of hands in the house and as my mother often said you should never give to receive if you've any goodness in your heart."

She sniffs her disapproval, making me apologise quickly for insulting her kindness.

"Very well," she says, "Anyway, your accent is coming along nicely, you've obviously been practicing."

She's right as I've little else to do all day long.

Taking a small pitcher of milk and some bread and jam from her basket she hands them to me.

"Today's the day, Little Robin," she tells me, pulling out a different old dress, one of her own which she has altered and re-trimmed to avoid detection.

She has some clogs which look far too big but will suffice—leather boots would be a definite giveaway. Newspaper is already inside to resize them, but this matters little as they will be covered by the hem of my dress.

My nickname came about when she told me I reminded her of a tiny bird, my hair like fluffy red feathers as I appeared at the door after my fitful night's sleep on the sacking. I feel like my affectionate namesake at this moment; a little robin poised on the cusp of leaving their nest to venture into the unknown. Nerves surpass my hunger, but I try to eat the food she's taken the trouble to provide.

"I hope I'm ready, Martha, I'd hate to bring trouble to your door."

I use her first name often to become accustomed to it. I'm already rehearsing the part of her cousin and must sound and act convincingly.

"You'll be fine. You're far from home so you can reinvent yourself and your story is straightforward enough to not trip up. Shall we run through it once more to be on the safe side?"

I nod even though I know it as well as The Lord's Prayer I learnt in school, never to be forgotten.

"So, you were widowed by your husband who died of the Asiatic flu like so many, and you found yourself bereft and pregnant. The master won't be asking you any questions and you'll rarely come across him, so don't fret."

I'm thankful for small mercies. I'll need some time to settle into my duties.

"Do you like Mr Mallerby?" I ask.

She pulls a hairbrush from the bottom of her basket. Without asking permission she unties my unruly plait and brushes my hair with skilful hands which doesn't make me feel uncomfortable. She's very motherly by nature making me wonder about her past.

"Your hair is only a few shades darker than my mother's. Hers was the colour of honey, whilst yours is more like a gleaming copper," she says.

She doesn't speak for a moment perhaps reliving memories of a time gone by.

"The master is a quiet man. I've worked for him many years, in fact since I was fourteen but truth be told I know little of him other than what I've found out from the comings and goings of domestic life. I don't mind him being elusive so much because it allows me to get on with my work without anybody breathing down my neck.

She admires her handiwork before putting the brush back in the basket.

"I somehow know he values me but only by his manner towards me as he's not one for compliments. I think you can tell if somebody likes you or not without them saying a word. The mistress is away at her mother's, so aside from Mr Slater, the butler, there's only me in the house nowadays. He wouldn't want to lose me because I work hard and keep my nose clean and I used this to our advantage in getting him to agree to you staying for a while to give me a hand with the chores."

I didn't realise there would be a Mrs Mallerby as I've never heard mention of her before. My stomach twists. I will be interacting with another woman of comparable standing to my own; vulnerable and exposed to more questioning than I would be with a man. Martha told me he lived alone, but I didn't think it only temporary. I had in my mind a bachelor or perhaps a widower as a woman would surely insist on a team of staff to help with the rituals of daily life.

"When is Mrs Mallerby due to return?" I ask.

I try to keep my voice light.

Pressing the final hairpin into my bun, Martha smiles at her own handiwork then shrugs dismissively.

"No idea. She's been away longer this time with only an occasional letter. The master never mentions her, and I haven't seen hide nor hair of her since the day she left. Her mother is very unwell is all I know. Right, you're all set, Renee. You'll do. So, be off with you now, and I'll meet you at the railway station as agreed at five o'clock. There's a train due in just after then so we can walk back to the hall together. The stationmaster will be having his tea, so he'll be none the wiser and nobody will be returning to the village at that hour. It's too early for some, too late for others."

What a detective she would make. She really has thought of everything and I'm thankful for her local knowledge. Folding the sacks which made up my uncomfortable bed I'm elated at the thought of being tucked up snugly in the servants' quarters of Mallerby Hall this very night. I change my dress in the time it takes for Martha to repack the basket with my things, and I look down at my new humble garb and clogs. I'm like a character in a play again. Perhaps this is exactly how I should tackle my new and strange situation.

Martha unbolts the huge wooden door, and I wait for her to nod then follow her across the ground floor of the factory, our clogs gently tip-tapping on the stone flags. Seemingly endless rows of neat wooden benches stand silent, ready to be brought to life by the clog makers in less than half an hour. I know from Martha's description three floors above will be laid out in a similar vein.

The world in these four walls will be different then: Vivid, vibrant, a bustling hotbed of northern enterprise, supplying the whole of Yorkshire and beyond. Millthwaite's Clog Factory is known far and wide.

Pushing her nose outside the front entrance, she checks the cobbled forecourt then beckons me towards her to make my escape to the woods at the rear.

I hesitate no more than a second, touching her arm by way of thanks. She smiles, still not saying a word just in case somebody should appear from nowhere.

The chilly air hits me and I think of the tiresome day ahead. All I can do is keep watch, rehearse my part, and wait.

Yet, as I wave farewell to 'Cousin Martha', I feel blessed.

I know she couldn't possibly feel any more like my family than she does at this very moment.

Chapter 3

My mind spins as I peer through the elaborate iron scrolls of the gates of Mallerby Hall. I'm so small and insignificant against the enormous proportions of the building.

I stand rooted, wondering how I can take the first step down the brick pathway to the rear entrance. I must soon carry out a preposterous façade, and one with deceit at the heart of it. I don't know if I have the nerve to pull it off.

Oh, my love, I miss you. I need you here by my side soothing me with encouraging words and squeezing my hand.

Yet, I know I must face life's troubles alone and I have no love to help me – not now.

"Here we are then, Renee, here's your new home," Martha says.

She smiles proudly, as though she's the rightful owner. I'm wearing a thicker shawl today which she brought to the railway station, another motherly gesture, and I clutch it around me now and sink briefly into the comfort it offers.

The last part of my disguise was a wedding ring which she slipped onto my finger. Who's wedding ring I wondered staring at it, imagining it must be her mother's. A ring had never occurred to me and though it's rather large, Martha said I will be able take it off soon when I start my domestic work. I cling to the ring as though my life depends on it. A wedding ring is a precious gift and not given away unless a person has died. The thought made me shiver.

Each curtain twitched in turn as we walked down The Avenue; the residents may as well have been standing on the doorstep with their arms folded. Curious eyes watching every step I took down the street so that I found it impossible to hold my head up, which is odd when nobody here knows the first thing about me.

Mallerby Hall is a good five-minute walk past The Avenue, standing solemnly in isolated grandeur surrounded by well-tended grounds. It is befitting of a man of Mr Mallerby's standing but I can't help thinking it's far too vast for one couple and two servants.

Martha said he wouldn't be at home for two hours or more so now is as good a time as any to make my entrance.

I heave a silent sigh and trudge behind her to the back door. This unassuming servants' entrance is now the gateway to my new life.

Martha deserves nothing but my gratitude and this is precisely what she will receive in the form of hard work and compliance, which is all I can offer.

I cross the threshold and see a smartly dressed man in a dark suit. I assume this is Mr Slater, the butler, poised to go up the scullery steps with a pair of polished black leather shoes in hand. His white hair is moulded like a velvet riding hat. He looks impeccable.

"Mr Slater, this is my cousin Renee who I was telling you about. Renee this is Mr Slater, Mr Mallerby's butler and you will address him as Mr Slater at all times."

His eyes travel up, then down me briefly but thankfully he shows no indication of seeing through our ruse. He has an air of snootiness one associates with butlers and I feel certain his eyes rest on my stomach a little longer than is appropriate. Perhaps my imagination has become a little overactive of late.

"How do you do, Mrs Robson," he says, inclining his head slightly to spoil the perfectly straight alignment of his posture.

I search for the very first line of my performance.

"Very well, thank you, Mr Slater," I say, doing my best to flatten my vowels the way Martha primed me.

My mouth is dry, and I dare not say any more for fear of falling at the first hurdle. Less is definitely more in terms of conversation.

Martha swiftly interrupts the lengthening silence, informing Mr Slater she will show me to my new living quarters before making a start on dinner. I can feel his eyes still upon me as I follow her down the corridor, making my legs quiver slightly. I'm starting to wonder if he has suspicions and knows already that I'm an imposter in the way that everyone instinctively knows another's station in a household. I'm poised to be called back for interrogation.

But it never comes.

My new sleeping arrangement in the cellar is like a palace in comparison to my recent quarters. Martha has been thoughtful enough to light a fire and the warmth welcomes me as soon as I walk in. The room houses two black iron beds, two identical wooden bedside tables and one wardrobe, all in dark-toned wood, perhaps walnut or yew. The furniture is fine quality, I suspect hand me downs from upstairs and I wonder if it was the same for our servants at home.

Don't think of home, Serena, not now.

How long is it since Martha shared her room with someone? I want to ask but it's too soon to pry.

"I've cleared one side of the wardrobe for your … things. Don't worry, we have a small allowance annually at Whitsuntide for new clothes but as May is a while away yet, Mr Slater says I'm to arrange a trip for your uniform along with one new coat, dress and hat for church. Now, won't that be exciting?"

"It certainly will," I say fixing a smile quickly in place.

Tears are stinging the back of my eyes and I'm trying my best not to let them spill. How I want to let the tears fall, to weep tears of self-pity for how my circumstances have been reduced so drastically. For how I must now rely on the kindness of strangers.

Instead, I swallow them down so I don't alarm Martha, knowing I will forever be indebted to this lady. She willingly and happily shares the little she has, and I am humbled.

Perching on my bed, she does the same on her own, watching me as my eyes scour the room to take in my unfamiliar surroundings. My eyes fall on the eiderdown, and I fight the urge to lay my head on it.

"I imagine you'd like to know who last slept in that bed," she says.

I only stare at her.

"It was my mother, some five years ago. Your quiet nature reminds me of her," she pauses, her head leaning to one side, "you know, sometimes I think people are sent to fill a void though you might think this silly."

Smiling weakly, I shake my head. I have been thinking the very same about my new companion. By the soft expression on her face, I have a hard act to follow with her mother but I'm content to try and fill a void for Martha for however long I can.

Getting to her feet she takes off her coat and hangs it in the wardrobe.

"Right, tea and cake, I think, then a quick look around. After that we must get down to business. There's a lot to learn so I hope you're a quick learner, by heck but I do."

We chuckle together, and as I hang my new shawl on the back of the door, I realise I've never considered the question. Yet if I don't learn the ropes quickly, I'll be on the streets or even in the workhouse.

I'm not sure at this moment which would be worse.

*

I don't recognise my own hands and feet. I've deliberately coarsened my lily-white hands in the days before my arrival here and my feet are raw simply from wearing the ill-fitting wooden clogs. How do people wear these things I wonder, but no-one I've met complains. I've been promised two new pairs of the correct size from Millthwaite's as soon as possible, but I can barely hide the wince which accompanies every step.

Martha said my main role is to help in the kitchen and keep the house fires burning to begin with. I'm to be introduced briefly to Mr Mallerby after dinner at his request and haven't to worry as she'll accompany me upstairs. I must not speak unless I'm spoken to.

How nice it would be not to worry when for years I seem to have done nothing else.

"Renee, the master is ready to see you now," Mr Slater says.

He's just returned from serving Mr Mallerby's brandy in the drawing room and his formal tone makes it sound like an official proclamation.

I think of Mr Mallerby upstairs. To eat alone every evening must be a lonely affair though after two years I expect he's grown accustomed to it.

My hands are shaking so I clasp them together in front of me as we take the long walk up the stairs and down the carpeted hallway. Mr Slater knocks twice on the sitting room door as I take long breaths through my nose, seeking composure.

"Come," signals an authoritative voice from beyond.

Martha smiles, encouraging me and I head to take my place centre stage.

Sir, may I introduce Mrs Renee Robson, Miss Wainwright's cousin and our new housemaid," Mr Slater says, stepping to one side.

I head towards Mr Mallerby's chair offering a small curtsey. As I raise my eyes they widen, and I must lower them immediately. This is not the picture of him I had formed in my mind.

"Good evening, Renee, I'm pleased to make your acquaintance," he says.

"Thank you, sir," I say, "I'm obliged to you for allowing me to work here."

My cheeks burning I'm certain this is not just from the heat of the room.

"I'm sure it will have been nice to reunite with your cousin under the circumstances. I hope you find your sleeping arrangements comfortable." He hesitates, "May I offer my condolences for your loss."

He's being far too sympathetic to a lowly servant, and I'm not in the correct frame of mind for sympathy. How long this day has been.

"You're very kind, sir," I manage to say.

I'm unable to hold his gaze which is full of compassion. This only tweaks my conscience so much I'd like to run from the room. I look at Martha quickly, grateful when she steps in.

"We won't take up any more of your time, sir," she says, "Thank you for seeing us and we bid you a good evening."

"If there is anything you need, please don't hesitate to ask Slater. Good evening to you both," Mr Mallerby says.

He's smiling gently and I think what a true gentleman he appears. When I look away, I continue to see his black-as-coal hair waving from his strong features. The portrait bathing in candlelight in the alcove does not do him justice.

"Mr Mallerby seems very kind, somehow I can sense it," I comment to Martha.

We're back in the safety of the kitchen and Mr Slater has retired for the night. She places the kettle on the range for our cocoa.

"Yes, that's a fair description. He and the mistress were very kind to me after my mother died, paying for a funeral and even attending themselves. He couldn't have made you any more welcome tonight, and I'm relieved," she smiles, "for both of us."

"I think it especially kind of him to take me on when I'm having a baby—generous to a fault is what I say."

Martha sits down in the chair by the range, and I join her in the seat opposite, removing my clogs with a sigh of relief. I notice she's fallen quiet and seems to be deliberately avoiding looking my way.

"About that," she says, "He doesn't entirely know about the baby just yet, Renee."

My heart plummets.

"By entirely, I assume you mean not at all."

She takes a sip of her cocoa pretending she didn't hear me whilst I begin to panic. My days in this beautiful house must surely be numbered.

Kindly he may be, but Mr Mallerby will not appreciate being taken for a fool.

Slumping in my chair I wrap my hands around my stomach like a protective shield. I will soon be all my baby has in the world again.

Oh, Martha, I think feeling quite sick, we've been fools ourselves to even consider trying to pull the wool over everybody's eyes in this house.

What on earth have we done?

Chapter 4

The last three weeks at the hall have been a flurry of learning my new station in life, learning new skills and learning how not to let my new persona slip. Just when I think I've got to grips with one thing, there's another. It seems like every day presents a different challenge, and I'm shamed by how much I took my former cossetted life for granted.

What I would have considered once to be the minutia of life at Walton Manor is, I've since learned, somebody else's entire life.

We had a full team of staff then but from conversations with Martha I understand the Mallerby family haven't been living in the lap of luxury for very long. Papa's money came from coal, wealth which had been handed down for generations, but Mr Mallerby's father founded Millthwaite's. He was a man from humble beginnings, uncomfortable adhering to the trappings of aristocracy and in turn, considering a team of staff an unnecessary extravagance. His son has clearly followed suit.

Where once my days would have begun with a breakfast tray presented to me in bed or at weekends, in the grand dining room; now, I am the one preparing the fare. I rise with Martha at half past five to make a start and must be grateful for an extra hour on a weekend.

"The master gets up with the larks, so we need to make sure we're up afore him. We must be ahead of the game cleaning and warming the rooms," she told me the first morning.

The first week she needed to rouse me as I was so tired, but now I'm in a routine of my own, the hidden rhythms of my body fully adjusted. Work clothes hide the growing roundness of my midriff though I don't know for how much longer. Martha keeps a watchful eye, so I don't give away our secret before she finds the right moment to tell Mr Mallerby.

I have seen him only twice and, on both occasions, it was when I was stoking his fire on an evening. Most nights I've managed to avoid him as he works in his study until late not wishing to be disturbed.

He waltzed into the room last evening startling me so much I dropped the coal tongs on the hearth tiles with a loud clatter. He was as flustered as I was, quickly apologising for taking me unawares.

"I'm sorry to disturb you, sir, I shan't be a moment," I said.

In my panic I momentarily dropped my local accent. He only stood staring at me without a word, so I thought at first that he'd seen my pregnancy bump and I'd been caught out. When he finally came out of his stupor, he tightened his housecoat around his waist and took his customary seat in the winged leather chair by the fire. I had polished the chair only hours before, as per Martha's instructions. It made me think of my old life which I can't help but miss often.

The crackle of the fire was the only sound in the silence and though I knew it was wrong I couldn't help but break it.

"I'm grateful to my cousin," I told him, "And to you for putting a roof over my head."

My mind went to papa. He will be at home now, I thought, with Moira, my stepmother. She might perhaps be playing the piano, or they may be reading together in the parlour. I wondered if Mr Mallerby had such a life with his wife or if he had always worked the same long hours as he does now.

Does he miss his wife? Is papa missing me? I can't imagine what excuse he and Moira have given for my absence. They may have said I'm visiting a sick grandmother in Dorset or some such nonsense to fend off the rumours. They won't want to lose face, especially with papa's business colleagues. Whatever the reason they thought of, I am sure I am gone never to return, and they will hope I will be forgotten in time. Our circle is small enough for them to have their wish eventually.

I drifted too long, I realised and when I looked up Mr Mallerby's face was pained with worry, perhaps thinking he may have upset a grieving widow still adapting to a life without her husband. I felt backed into a corner.

"I will leave you in peace now, sir, and bid you a good evening," I said, my smile no doubt too broad, so I will have looked like I was wearing the mask of a clown.

His mouth opened and closed slightly, so I thought he may have been about to say something but thought better of it. When he didn't, I was panicked then by the terrible silence.

"Yes, good evening, Renee," he said finally.

Taking a small sip from his brandy glass he reached for his crisp newspaper from the side table.

I caught his reflection in the glass of the door as I went to leave. If I'm not mistaken his eyes were not reading at that moment.

Instead, they were following me intently until I disappeared out the room.

Chapter 5

If it wasn't for Rowena, I think I would have taken leave of my senses over the torment I've suffered these last few years.

How I treasure our friendship and her home is a welcome escape. At home, life is a pendulum swinging from drama to monotony and Wentworth House is my sanctuary. I stay at every opportunity.

My stomach is never entirely free of a tightness at home. A sense of foreboding follows me around the rooms and I'm unable to shake it, even in my own bedroom. Privacy has never been at the top of my stepmother's list of priorities.

"I think we should face facts, Serena; your stepmother is unhinged. I think she's jealous of you… the green-eyed monster has taken control of her."

We're both languishing side by side on the four-poster bed of the guest room. Rowena's mother says I should consider it my room. When she mentioned it in passing, she will never know how much it made me feel as though I'm part of their family. I've come to understand being part of a family is more important when you've lost it. I hadn't felt that pleasure in so long.

When I'm here I'm as neat as a pin and quiet as a mouse, falling over myself to not give them a reason to want me to leave … or not to come. But exactly how long it will continue I can't be sure. I'm skating on very thin ice.

I swing my forearm over my eyes and try to block out the unwelcome image of my stepmother's face. If ever she bothers herself to look at me, she carries a certain expression, one she reserves only for me.

"I make sure I keep from under Moira's feet but still she seeks me out purely to find fault. Unless papa is home, of course."

"Underhandedness is the worst kind of nastiness in my book," Rowena says, fiddling with one of the many rags tied in her hair. Tomorrow her poker-straight dark hair will be cascading in curls down her back. This is the secret to her pride and joy.

Her father and mine are on the board at the Brighouse & Huddersfield Bank which means occasionally her mother and my stepmother's paths must cross at functions. After their first meeting, the door was swung back widely for me at Wentworth.

"Moira makes me uneasy," Rowena's mother told her in an unguarded moment, "I can see beneath the show well enough. If only Serena's father could see through her, but he seems blind to it."

"You know, I'm not sure if mother is right," Rowena says now, "I wonder if your papa is blind to her ways or blinded by her—there's a difference. Moira knew what she wanted, and she simply took him without a second thought for anyone but herself. She's cunning but then your father was lonely and so I imagine he prefers to live a life of pretence rather than a life of solitude. I often think how your dear mama will be spinning in her grave."

She takes my hand by her side gently. Such a tender touch that speaks volumes to me without the need for words.

Once such a comment would have made me hold my breath to stop the tears but after three years without mama the pain is now a dull ache. The twist of my heart when her name is mentioned has finally lessened.

We grow quiet and I take a moment to relive the events of this evening's gathering. Rowena's brother, Dicken has a friend staying from his university days. Timothy is quite taken with Rowena, and I can see why he would be. She looked so elegant tonight in her new satin gown, playing the piano whilst playing a game of cat and mouse with their eyes. Timothy's fairness compliments her dark colouring; I often tell her how much I would love her black hair, but she insists my auburn tresses are what every girl wants. We both agree one is never satisfied with one's lot in life.

"Serena, I think my sister may be a touch smitten with the newcomer, what say you?" Dicken said teasing her on our way up to bed.

He was a tread ahead, turning around to talk to me. His black hair, the same colour as his sister's was not quite so immaculate as it was at the beginning of the evening and his top button was undone. Dicken always has a way of making me feel like I'm the only person in the room when he speaks to me. It can make me a little awkward under the scrutiny, especially when his fiancée, Anabelle is in the room. I sense her watching me, watching him, so I try very hard not to, but then my awkwardness makes me appear very odd in her company.

"I think you may be right, Dickie, she couldn't seem to tear her eyes away," I said light-heartedly, trying as always to pull off a carefree persona.

I've somehow always wanted him to think me an interesting, lively person worthy of his attention.

"Oh, you two, such partners in crime. I was fascinated by his lazy eye squinting my way is all."

We all laughed on the way to our respective rooms. It wasn't long however before Rowena made her way to my room for our regular bedtime rundown of the day's events.

Running and jumping on the bed in her long white nightgown, she flopped on the pillows with a sigh.

"Dicken's right, of course, I am quite taken with Timothy. My only fear is he'll think I'm chasing his money, and his title. His father is Viscount Rothbury you know."

"Oh really, I don't think you've ever mentioned that before, Weenie."

She pushes me playfully and we laugh together. My best friend would be a prize for any man, though she doesn't know it. Beautiful, accomplished, clever, witty – she has the perfect demeanour and though we might be considered "new money" by the gentry, her family's fortune would bridge that gap, I'm sure.

"I'll be glad when the wedding's over," Rowena says now, "I'm sick of hearing about it, Anabelle talks of nothing else," she pauses and turns her head my way. She briefly looks unsure whether to go on, "Do you think she's a good match for Dickie?"

I try not to give an opinion on any matter at Wentworth. I prefer to stay neutral and benign in my approach to conversation in case my words should be misconstrued. I would hate to cause offence.

"More importantly, do you think so?" I ask.

I've come to find this distraction technique useful in many situations. I stare at the perfect folds of the four-poster bed canopy above our heads as she gives the question some thought.

"I find her to be one of those girls who would marry anybody who asked her," she says eventually, "I may be doing her a disservice, but I don't think she truly loves Dickie. He too seems apathetic but perhaps I live with my head in the clouds in regard to love and all its connotations. Mother says so anyway."

I notice the candle is burning low and the fire in the grate is dying to just a glow. I listen to the wind a moment in the cosy setting before my mind wanders to other concerns. I find myself unable to have a valid opinion on her brother's situation.

Sadly, I know only too well Dicken doesn't love Anabelle.

I know because Dicken is in love with me … and he has been for the whole of the last three years.

Even if I should want to, this unnerving fact alone makes it impossible for me to comment.

Chapter 6

"Me, Martha?" I ask, "But I thought you were the only person he trusts."

I shake my head, confused about the request which has been made from out of the blue.

"Well, he said it would save me a job if you could nip over once a day knowing how much I have on my plate. It looks like you've made a good impression. But then again, being my cousin and all, you're obviously from fine stock."

Martha laughs but I can't join in as the comment only highlights our deception. I'm constantly trying to push it to the back of my mind but it's getting more difficult each day that goes by. I slide my plate away suddenly lacking an appetite.

"He must be told about the baby before too long, Martha. This is at least one thing I can be honest about."

She leaves the table to dish up sponge pudding then covers it with a layer of thick custard. I feel sick at the sight though this is nothing to do with her cooking. Many things make me nauseous, particularly smells, cabbage being by far the worst.

"It's tricky because I know we should have told him from the start," she says, placing a bowl in front of me then sitting down to join me, "But in my head, I was thinking we should take one step at a time. I admit you're showing more now, but then I wonder if this is because I know you're pregnant."

I look down at my stomach then pick up my spoon to push the pudding around, unable to eat it.

"Perhaps I should tell him tonight. I'll say I didn't tell you about the baby, so you're not implicated. It will be far better to face the consequences sooner rather than later and Mr Slater should be told too."

Martha's cheeks colour but then she smiles suddenly. I wonder what she's about to say.

"He's sweet on you is our Mr Slater, you know. But I bet with a face like yours you've never been short of admirers."

Her confession wasn't what I was expecting at all.

"He never is, I haven't seen any sign of it," I say in a tone that expresses surprise and disbelief at the same time.

"No, that's because you don't realise how bonny you are, my dear Little Robin. I know Mr Slater and he's not quite himself, shall we say."

I put my spoon down in the bowl and sit back in my chair.

"Well, he won't be sweet on me after he finds out. Oh, Martha what a predicament I've dragged you into and you had such a quiet life before I arrived."

She laughs softly as she concentrates on the last scrapings in her bowl.

"I've had a bellyful of quiet, thanks all the same. You were sent to me that morning, I know it like I know tomorrow's Sunday. Make no mistake, I've enjoyed you working here these last few weeks.

The sentiment behind her words makes me cover her hand with my own across the table. She glances up at me and clears her throat.

"I'd just like to say if you ever want to talk about how you came to be in the circumstances you find yourself in, then I'll be only too happy to lend a willing ear."

I drop my head back with a sigh.

"Honestly, there's nobody else I'd rather take into my confidence, but I'm still trying to come to terms with everything that's happened. One day I'll be ready, and you'll be the first person to hear it."

Stroking the back of her veiny hand with my thumb I look up at the face I wake to each morning. This endearing face that has been getting me through each day.

I find a weary smile. I just can't drag her into this web of trouble I find myself in.

Not Martha.

*

Fatigue is becoming more of a problem of late. The extra cleaning at Millthwaite's isn't helping but my only option is to keep going then sleep like the dead at night.

At six o'clock prompt and in darkness I start my walk through the woods to the factory. The nights are drawing in and the weather is decidedly wintry. My shawl offers little protection from the iciness tonight; the time has come to wear my wool coat if it will fit.

Martha cleans the office on a morning after breakfast, and I take the evening shift when I've finished helping her with supper. I really can't imagine how she managed before I arrived.

Candlelight flickers through the opaque glass of the window to Mr Mallerby's office. I'd been hoping all the way here he might have left for the day. My heart falls.

After checking the state of my dress and clogs, I knock on the oak panelled door of the office. There's no answer, so I try once more, finally relieved to hear his command to enter.

"I apologise, I didn't realise the time, Renee," he says when I appear around the door.

Is it my imagination or does he look a little flustered? I'm used to him exhibiting full control, the epitome of calm but he's shuffling his papers together a little too manically and his pallor is greyer than usual. He places the pile in the top drawer of his desk and locks it with a small key which he then slips into his waistcoat pocket.

"I assume Wainwright has informed you of the tasks in hand for the evening cleaning duties," he says, his composure restored.

This office and adjoining meeting rooms are clearly a symbol of wealth and status, decorated to impress and I can't help but notice the opulence of the décor as I head to his desk. The look is similar to papa's gentlemen's club; I've studied the photograph many times on the wall of his study, the one showing him sitting with two late colleagues from the bank.

Mr Mallerby's face is stretched into a broad smile, but it stops short of his eyes, so the sight is rather off-putting. He's certainly acting out of character this evening and I can only assume it's because we're in a work rather than a home setting.

"She has indeed told me, sir," I say quickly, "I'll make a start and get from under your feet."

My accent is becoming more convincing by the day, Serena Wilton-Robbins is disappearing steadily into the mist of yesterday.

"Well then, I shall head home for my supper. I bid you farewell for the time being and I'll see you later this evening.

I heave a breath. This is it I think, this is the moment to tell him about the baby. Whatever his reaction, I must do it now or I may never. I open my mouth to speak but the words stick fast, perspiration climbing its way up my cold back. Panicked, I stare into his eyes; eyes which are once more filled with concern. It's too overwhelming.

Suddenly, he scoots around the desk asking, "Are you quite alright, Mrs Robson, you don't look at all well?"

He's rushing towards me and I'm backing away, my legs not feeling like they belong to me. The sound of the pendulum swinging in the grandfather clock is steadily being drowned out by the pounding blood in my ears.

"I …I must…" is a far as I get with an explanation.

The last thing I process with my conscious mind is Mr Mallerby's arms reaching out towards me. No, I can't do this I think as I fall like a dead weight straight into them.

Chapter 7

"What's bothering you, Serena?"

The question irritates me immediately. What's bothering me? Nothing at all Dickie except perhaps the love of my life marrying somebody else in one month's time, and that I'm to be rubbed out of his life like an etching which no longer suits the artist. He tried it, but it wasn't quite right.

What could possibly be bothering me, Dicken?

But instead, I say, "I wish things could be different."

The ridiculous understatement irritates me even more. I am repressed, unable to voice an opinion due to the fear of repercussions.

An old shepherd's hut in the fold of the moors has become our meeting place. I think of it as our little port in a storm. We meet here as often as we can, the schedule largely revolving around Dicken's work and the weather. The way to the hut is overgrown, far away from any regular paths so we can be sure nobody will come across us. Even so, we're always sure to arrive and leave separately.

Moira has repressed me; I was a different person with mama. We used to chat about the mundane and the important things in equal measure, free to support and challenge each other at will, yet we never had a cross word in all my eighteen years. She was my stay. I wonder what she would make of Dicken and if she would think him weak for not challenging his parents about their choosing him a wife. Do I think him weak? I close my eyes to the question.

"Believe me, I wish things were different too, Serena but my path has been set in stone since I was a young boy. Anabelle's parents and my own have been planning this forever as you know."

There's still a part of me which likes to think that at the eleventh hour he will back out of the wedding unable to consider a life without me.

"Dicken, you will have to make a choice before too long. I hope you don't think you can continue to see me after your marriage to Anabelle."

We're sitting outside, enjoying the spring sunshine, though it's still a little chilly. I see his face dart my way from the corner of my eye as I look toward the view, but his lack of a rebuttal tells me so much about his assumption of our future path. Oh, the audacity of him; disappointment hits me like a tidal wave.

But it's all too late.

When the cold weather was still upon us, less than two weeks ago I was struggling with his indecision. I tried to jolly myself out of the mood by bringing along tea to drink in fine porcelain cups I'd brought from Walton Manor just for the fun of it. However, I soon found out fun is not something which can be manufactured. The upcoming wedding was looming large but going behind Rowena's back has been the biggest cross to bear. That Saturday, for the first time I was unable to put on a brave face.

"My darling," Dicken said pulling me from my chair to sit on his knee, "We'll work it out, I'm sure of it, because a life without you is no life at all."

He stroked my hair as I leant against his chest. I should have stopped to think about the meaning behind his words, but they seemed so genuine and heartfelt I was certain he would be calling the wedding off.

Lifting my chin gently he gazed into my eyes before kissing me gently on my lips… then my eyelids, my cheek, neck. His tenderness convinced me I'd never been closer to this man who made me laugh, who made me feel important, valued. Who made me live from one precious meeting to the next.

His hand slid to my breast, and I gasped from surprise and the pleasure of it. My mind was now far away from the turmoil, sinking into a new sensation until I could think of nothing else. Unbuttoning my dress his hands touched the bare flesh of my thigh making me bolt and gasp, as his fingers climbed higher and higher. Part of me wanted him to stop but that part was no longer in control and I allowed him to touch me in a way which made a small, strange sound escape me.

"My beautiful girl," he said, his face in my hair, "My wonderful titian goddess, how I've longed for this, how I've dreamt about it."

He pushed my hand against the strain of his britches, moaning as he nudged me from his knee. Then with his back against the cabin wall he pulled my underwear down and swiftly lifted me around his waist, my legs astride him. I clawed at the moss and stone at the side of his head as thrusting his hips, he took what I offered, what I truly wished to give him in that moment. There was nothing else but him, the wanting of him, the pleasure of him.

"Dicken, my love, I've wished our bodies to be as one, I've needed this too long. You must know I am completely yours."

Our bodies did our bidding, shuddering with pleasure, joined as I hoped. I became his, exhilarated by the union.

Afterwards, we sat together, arms folded around each other. We stared at the snowy scene from the tiny cabin window and relived the memory of what had just happened for the first time. There were no regrets.

But now, I realise our thoughts in that moment could not have been more different.

Until today I've relived the pleasure of our lovemaking almost like an obsession. But the memory has now been sullied. He has sullied it.

Spring has shown itself, but the sunshine does little to warm me.

"Do you think so little of me you would keep me as a secret lover?" I say, "To be in love with a man who is engaged is a grievous deception, loving a man who is married and breaking the sanctity of marriage vows quite another."

Casting my eyes in his direction he looks away as though my gaze burns him.

I have a physical pain, contrasting with the chirruping happy song of the moorland finch eerily so I can barely breathe. As we sat watching the snow that day it seems I was planning a future together whilst he was planning a future where he had both a wife and a mistress.

I turn my head away to wipe a tear.

Dicken Carter-Knowles has broken my heart.

Chapter 8

Scrambling from my chair I'm gently pushed back down in my seat by the same hands which saved me from a fall.

"Whoa, there, I'm afraid you mustn't think of going anywhere at present."

Mr Mallerby's hair is out of place, his pallor now changed from grey to ashen. But he has taken control of the situation and in this moment I'm glad of it. I've never fainted before in my life.

"I apologise, sir, I don't know what came over me, I'll make a start on the boardroom right away."

I'm aware that I'm gabbling, shaking my head slightly to try and focus on the wall behind his head. I must look like I'm losing my mind.

With one hand still on my forearm he raises the other to protest.

"Renee, as your employer I see it as my duty to be sure you are well enough to work. Tomorrow is soon enough for the cleaning to be done, but for tonight I must escort you home."

I remember now why I fainted. What should be my next move? Should I feign illness or tell him the truth of the matter.

"I'm having a baby."

The baldness of the statement makes him stand upright and take a step backwards as though he's been punched. I too am shell-shocked, the words spilling out before I could check them.

He only looks at me a moment, before saying quietly: "I see." "I'm sure you must have been very anxious about telling me." He pauses, "perhaps this is why you fainted."

Oh, don't look at me like that I think, running a hand down my face.

"Perhaps," I say, "I… I was very worried. I'm sorry for not telling you before, but of course I understand that you will expect me to leave now."

There was never going to be a right time to tell him about my pregnancy. Time was ticking, and though I'm fearful for the future, part of me is relieved to speak the truth, or at least some of it.

"Renee, you know little of me, but would you think me so callous as to throw a pregnant widow out onto the street?"

My hand goes to my mouth. Did he really say I could stay on at Mallerby Hall for the time being? Though the knot in my stomach is unravelling slightly I must check it.

"I'm certainly grateful to you, Mr Mallerby, but it would be far too much of an imposition. I'm almost a stranger to you after all."

His eyes are upon me as I realise too late that Renee's mask is slipping again. He leans his head to one side.

"Yes, you are indeed almost a stranger," he says, looking at me so intently I shift in my seat, "but Wainwright has been a loyal servant to me all her adult life, and her mother before, so doing right by her family would be no less than she deserves. Regardless, I could never turn my back on a woman in your circumstances, a woman in need of refuge and shelter."

My heart is beating in my mouth, so palpable is my relief. My new life may be built on quicksand but it appears I'm safe for the foreseeable future. Oh, the joy of being thrown an unexpected lifeline, I can't wait to tell Martha.

"I'll make sure we keep out of your way, sir, be sure of it, you won't know we're there. My work won't suffer either, I'll work even harder to repay your kindness."

He smiles ruefully on his way back to his desk.

"From what I gather, babies aren't often quiet, nor are they meant to be. However, I suspect Martha will be only too happy to help."

A weight has been lifted and Martha will be delighted. It may not be forever but it's more than I could ask.

"Come Renee, tonight you shall ride home with me in my carriage. After what has happened, I think it best if you go straight to bed and I shall ask the doctor to attend on you at his earliest convenience."

This is too much. I scrabble my feet, saying, "No, sir, I'm perfectly fine, I'll see a doctor in due course but for now I'm sure a little rest will be enough."

His eyes lower to my stomach, then he looks quickly away. What a shock he will have had.

"As you wish but I'd prefer it you didn't wait too long," he says.

Putting on his hat he grabs his cane before taking his coat from the stand.

"I think you should wear your warm coat now the weather has turned but wear mine for tonight," he says placing it around my shoulders. It's far too big in every direction and drags on the floor as I walk. "You are in the midst of a very difficult time in your life, but rest assured you and your child have a roof over your heads. Distress is not good for a baby."

I lift his coat as I walk behind him into the courtyard. For two pins I could crumple in a heap to the floor again but this time it would be in a flood of tears.

43

I must find strength, for a mother must be strong for her child. As my own mother was strong for me, especially at the end.

Jenkinson, the coachman, jumps down from his seat as we approach. The horses are waiting as patiently and obediently as ever and make me think of home and then of Wentworth House, but for once I'm not homesick. I'm going to my new home to see Martha, and I have good news to share at last. We can sleep easier tonight.

Jenkinson's eyebrows lift slightly when I appear from behind Mr Mallerby with his coat around my shoulders.

"Renee is a little unwell, Jenkinson. She will accompany me back to the hall in the carriage this evening… and please take it gently man, we must not be shaken from our seats."

"Of course, very good, sir," he says, hesitating before holding out his hand to help me into the cab, clearly perplexed at my special treatment.

Mr Mallerby sits opposite me and holds out a rug for my knees. The evening has turned foggy and dampness pervades our clothes. We sit in silence for a while as we skirt the brooding stillness of Lady Well Wood before being bathed in the yellow light of The Avenue and back to the hall. The elegant, terraced villas are glowing and I catch sight of some families ensconced by their firesides. I have a sense of calm, of peace— a sensation which has eluded me for months, years even.

The sight of the hall through the evening mist is a welcome one.

"Martha will enjoy fussing and clucking around you like a mother hen, I imagine," he says with a low laugh.

"Yes, I think I'm in good hands," I say.

I have a question which has been bothering me. I'm hesitant to ask it but this seems an appropriate time.

"Your generosity warms my heart, sir, but I can't help but wonder if your wife would be so accommodating should she return."

Shuffling in his seat I'm startled when his mouth tightens and sets so his face looks like a cast. It seems I've overstepped the mark.

He stares out of the window of the carriage, his face in profile expressionless. We sway to the trot of the horses as I wish I could swallow my words back down again.

He doesn't move and I can tell his mind is far away.

"My wife will never return," is all he says.

Chapter 9

Watching the swish and the swing of a beautiful bridesmaid dress would ordinarily be one of life's finest pleasures but in these circumstances I must tread carefully.

"Rowena, you will outshine the bride, and this will not sit well with Anabelle."

As she twirls in my direction the dress follows to settle about her legs.

"If it was up to Dickie, I'm sure you would be a bridesmaid but of course this is only her ladyship's decision."

She pulls down the corners of her mouth with disdain, crossing her eyes and I can't help but smile at my friend's antics. It's fair to say her sister-in-law to be is a thorn in her side.

"Well, she hasn't spared any expense with your dress, the peach velvet of the bodice is just exquisite," I say, swiftly changing the subject.

In just two days' time, Dicken and Anabelle are to be married in York Minster close to her parent's home. The day will no doubt be full of pomp and ceremony so typical of Anabelle: the wedding of the decade, never mind the year and no expense has been spared by her father with the whole event. She's an only daughter as am I, but our weddings will be quite different fairy tales if I should ever marry. I'd rather not think about it.

"I must go home and see papa; two weeks have gone by since my last visit and I need to collect my dress."

Thoughts of home dampen my mood further. My visits are getting further and further apart and I find every excuse imaginable to stay away.

"Perhaps you could come back the same day and tell Moira you're needed to help with wedding preparations," Rowena says, slipping out of her dress.

Papa and Moira are to be guests at Dicken's wedding as our fathers are longstanding friends and colleagues at the bank. How the festive day looms rather than beckons but I've plenty to attend to before then. Sadly, it has nothing whatsoever to do with wedding preparations.

We join Rowena's mother in the garden for tea on the huge lawn. The table is laid with a lace tablecloth crammed with a feast of dainty sandwiches, cakes and scones meant to entice. I've little appetite at present so mealtimes have become particularly trying.

"Ah, girls, here you are. I hope your dress fits perfectly Rowena dear as we only have tomorrow for last-minute alterations if not. What did you think, Serena?"

Her mother's blue and white cotton dress is new I see, her parasol twirling elegantly between her fingers as she speaks. She is a true lady.

"Rowena looks a picture of perfection, Mrs CK," I reassure her.

"Splendid, well that's one less thing for me to worry about," she says.

She smiles happily and chooses a cucumber sandwich from the silver stand. Usually, Rowena's mother is a calming, motherly presence but I've been avoiding her of late. The strain of pretending all is well has been wearing me out.

"Are you going for your walk today?" Rowena's mother asks.

She's aging gracefully and Rowena gets her striking colouring from her mother. I always compare her to my dear mama and she comes a close second. Mama too never looked her years … until the end.

"Yes, I thought I might as the weather is so agreeable," I turn to Rowena now and raise my eyebrows, asking my usual unspoken rhetorical question. The answer is always the same.

"I'm going to have a lie down and read *Love & Friendship* which is very appropriate for the moment don't you think?" she says smothering a scone with butter, "Tramping the moors is not my idea of fun as you know, Serena."

I smile thinking today more than ever I'm glad Rowena detests walking. Perhaps if she didn't, I might not be in this predicament.

After tea I glance over my shoulder to see Rowena and her mother walking arm in arm towards the house then I head out through the kitchen garden to the back gate. The walled garden is a favourite spot to sit and read. Today the delicate scent of the sweet peas scrabbling up the wall fills my nostrils as I start up the hillside.

He told me he might not be able to join me today but I'm living in hope.

"Serena, it's difficult for me to get away as papa has already granted two weeks holiday after the wedding so we can … holiday on the south coast," he said last time we met.

He almost said honeymoon on the south coast but thought better of it, I think.

What will I do if he doesn't come? I lift my skirts higher to pick up speed, my ankles in danger from the divots and stones scattered along the path but I don't care. Time is fast running out.

Today I haven't brought any refreshments along with me, any silly little decadent whim to enhance our time together. Should he make an appearance there will be only one item on the agenda.

I wait for more than an hour at the rear of our hut: sitting then pacing in rotation. I would normally be enthralled by the view, the landscape donning new garb with the passing of each season.

His silent approach across the heather means I'm startled when he appears from nowhere. His expression is serious, suddenly making him look more mature, older even. I haven't noticed before.

Has he told Anabelle? He was adamant he would last time we met but I think I may already know the answer.

"What is it?" I ask, instinctively.

He lifts his trousers at the knee to sit by my side on the wooden bench we often share. Though he's staring straight ahead at the view, like me, I know he's not taking it in. Something is wrong.

"I shouldn't have come here today but I knew I must," he says.

My fears are being realised, and a panic is rising.

"I must talk to you, Dicken."

His head drops back, closing his eyes so he looks in pain.

"You're to have a baby, aren't you?" he says.

I take a sharp intake of breath, my jaw hanging.

"How do you know?"

He rakes a hand through his hair then turns his head to look at me.

"I thought at first you were upset about the wedding as you'd been acting out of character. But then Weenie mentioned in passing you'd been feeling unwell so I just had an inkling that you might be. I've been worried about it since that time we, you know. I pay more attention than you give me credit for sometimes."

Acting out of character; I pay attention, he says. Oh, why then are you marrying somebody else, Dicken, answer me that if you will.

"What will you do?" he asks.

I swing my face in his direction; the question winding me, though it shouldn't. My suspicions were well-founded, I know now I am not, indeed we are not, to be part of his future. My stomach is churning this way and that, my mind doing the same. I'm on my own; we're on our own. My life is to change but I must gain strength from somewhere and soon. I try to quash the alarm which is making me shiver from head to toe. Perhaps I am in shock.

Thoughts of what mama would do begin to soothe me slightly. What would she do I wonder. My dear mama would take a deep breath, gather her wits and think of a solid plan. Even now she is my guiding light in the darkness.

And all the while Dicken sits by my side wishing I was anywhere but by his side.

Somehow, I manage to stand to loom over him, placing him in my shadow. He hasn't said a word and his eyes remain pinned to the ground, unable to meet mine.

"I thought perhaps you were a man to at least consider stepping up to your responsibilities. I hoped you might surprise me … how silly of me."

How silly of me to think for a moment he might call off the wedding. To think he would ever be mine. Though he doesn't love Annabelle, this was never on his agenda, it's all suddenly so clear to me.

"You think I don't love you," he says, "That I've used you, but I haven't. I'm guilty of burying my head in the sand, I agree, I thought I could work everything out somehow. But I realise now the day is almost upon us that I don't know how to. I just don't know how to stop the wheel from turning.

Hope lifts my heart.

"I could help you. We could face it together if you're willing," I say.

His eyes stay fixed to the ground giving me my answer loud and clear. Hope has faded quicker than a rose in autumn.

I glare at him, the wind blowing my hair loose strand by strand, so it whips across my cheeks.

"I've realised too late how weak you are, Dicken," I say, pushing hair from my eyes, "but I'd be glad if you would answer me this: How can you possibly marry a woman, give up your life to a woman whom you do not love?"

Bending forward to rest his forearms on his thighs he moves his head from side to side.

"Look here Serena, I thought I didn't care about money and status, that love was all I needed—our love. Yet now there's a real possibility of losing everything I've discovered my reputation is important me. I can't say I like it about myself very much, but I can't deny who I am."

Only moments ago, I was sitting in the sunshine but now he's taken me by the hand and led me to a very dark place. He's gone already and left me here all on my own.

"I see so I'm to face the shame alone, is that it? You are to carry on with your life as if I never existed, as if *we* never existed."

I stare at the top of his head, the panic now threatening to take hold of me.

"I'm sorry, Serena. I shall miss you, but we haven't been living in the real world. Love can fade with the harsh realities of life and then I will be left with nothing not even the respect of my family."

"And what do you think will happen should I tell everyone who the father is," I say, the words cold and only half-meant, full of my own despair.

"Please Serena. I know I deserve no better but for the love we have shared I beg you not to. For then we are both damned for eternity."

A hollow laugh escapes me; I've heard enough from this man. He knows I won't do that, to break the hearts of those I love; Rowena, Papa, even Anabelle, they don't deserve it. No, the damage is done, and even if he changes his mind tomorrow, next year, the damage is irreparable.

I shall not lower myself to avenge him, however much he has hurt me.

Picking up my skirts I swing around and take the first step of my long walk back to Wentworth, knowing my days there are numbered. How I wished I had found out about his fiancée before he took my heart.

When I hear his voice calling after me, I don't even break my stride.

"If you need money, you only have to ask," he shouts.

Of all the things he could have said, this was certainly the worst.

I hold my head high and walk down the hill through the path we've trampled in the heather over the years, each step taking me steadily further from my hopes and dreams.

So now I have no choice but to face the harsh reality head on.

But I vow to myself that this is the last time Dicken Carter-Knowles will ever break my heart.

Chapter 10

"Never coming home. Are you sure they were his exact words; did he actually say the word 'never'?"

Nodding, I sit on the edge of my bed. I've had an emotional day and I'd much prefer for it to just come to an end.

"Well, blow me. Like I told you, as far as Mr Slater and me knew she was visiting her sickly mother. I half expected her to walk through the door any day."

Mrs Mallerby remains a mysterious, enigmatic figure. There are no portraits to study or a dress to set eyes on. I dust her room weekly, but her wardrobe doors are locked. Curiosity got the better of me and I couldn't help but check.

"What was she like?"

Martha lifts her eyes to the ceiling, no doubt trying to piece together the perfect description for me.

"The mistress was a fine-looking lady, blonde with delicate features. She was … is very pleasing to look at but not what you would call a straightforward person," she looks at me, "no, I think you must have misheard; I can't imagine she will *never* be setting foot in this house again."

I try to paint a picture in my mind from Martha's portrayal. I'm sure she and her husband will have made a handsome couple. Perhaps Mr Mallerby works such long hours because the house seems lonely and empty. I understand that feeling only too well.

"What do you mean by not straightforward?" I ask, my interest suddenly tweaked.

Taking her shoes off Martha sits with her feet up on the bed, her back against the propped pillows. The time is only just past nine o'clock, but we decided to retire early as we have so much to discuss.

I told Mr Slater about my situation when we were having supper, thinking it only fair. He should not be the only person in the household not to know. Although in his late thirties, the same as Mr Mallerby according to Martha, I would say he looks a good decade older. His hairstyle makes him look austere, and his moustache is too bushy.

"I see, well I offer you my congratulations, Renee," he paused, his expression telling me he'd just remembered something, "although I understand if you feel this may not be appropriate under the circumstances."

He realised then he meant because I'm supposedly widowed rather than a woman who has fallen from grace.

"Thank you, Mr Slater," I said, "no, you're quite right, this is news to celebrate."

I didn't add especially as I now have a roof over my head, instead I jumped up quickly to clear the dishes, keen to end the awkward interaction for both of us.

"The mistress was temperamental," Martha says now, "oh dear this will never do, she is temperamental. Her mood could swing like a pendulum some days and I don't think she ever went to bed in the same frame of mind as she woke up but I was used to her ways. We adapt to peoples' ways in service; we must adapt and quickly if we're to have any chance of keeping our job."

She rubs her hands up and down her swollen calves as I think how little rest time she has. We spend Sunday afternoons reading for a while when Mr Slater visits his mother, but this is her only break from the gruelling routine.

"Do you think they were in love?" I ask.

Curiosity still has a hold of me.

"In love? I know nothing of such things, Little Robin, I'm sure you would have been a better judge."

Laughing gently, she shakes her head as I slide from the bed to tidy our room. I'd rather not think about my heartbreak at present.

"So, apparently we're to move to the attic guest rooms, I can't quite believe it," she says.

"Nor can I, this has been quite a day, but you are the reason Mr Mallerby is being so supportive. He'd like to repay you for all you and your mother have done over the years."

As I pull my new coat from the wardrobe, I recall how Mr Mallerby's coat felt around my shoulders only hours ago. I felt warm, protected like I used to feel with papa when mama was alive. Like nothing bad could happen to me.

"Well, I just do my job the same as many others, nowt special."

He thought it best for us to move to the attic rooms as he said a cellar however comfortable, is no place for a mother-to-be and eventually a new-born baby. Two rooms on the third floor are to be allotted for us so Martha can be nearby. We went up to look at them before bed.

"I'll feel like a lady sleeping in here," she said.

Her expression was wistful as she took in the splendour of the bedroom through different eyes. The room is to be hers and hers alone.

"I've dusted this room along with the others for fifty years or more and now I'm to sleep here. It somehow doesn't seem right."

"I know it will seem odd for a while, Martha, but in time you'll get used to it. We can get accustomed to almost anything."

She knew what I was referring to and nodding thoughtfully, she shrugged and smiled, then walked to the far end of the room to open the door to a cupboard. She gestured with her head for me to join her and I squinted in the gloom.

"The master says you're to use this," she said.

I wasn't expecting to see a crib draped with a white lace cover. I reached to touch it almost to be sure it was real.

"I'm grateful to him but why is this in here?" I asked as we both stared at it.

"This crib was in and out of here too many times to mention. Three times a pregnancy was announced, and three times it ended in tears," she said.

Martha didn't look my way, she only continued to stare at the baby's crib, as though she was reliving that time.

How tragic, how cruel for this to happen to the couple. I remembered Mr Mallerby's faraway look when I asked about his wife. He misses her.

"Perhaps that's why she left; she will have been haunted, unable to overcome it. Such a loss is a terrible pain to bear, Martha."

"It is, you're right," she said, closing the door, "But why didn't the master follow her at least. I'm finding it all so difficult to understand."

As am I, I thought as we headed back downstairs.

Mr Mallerby appeared at the parlour door startling me.

"I thought you were to retire early, Renee," he said flatly.

I felt like an admonished child.

"We're just on our way now, sir," Martha said, pushing me gently from behind, "I'm grateful to you for our new sleeping arrangements."

Nodding, he closed the door as though he'd barely heard her.

Now I lay in bed staring at the ceiling. Martha fell asleep almost the moment her head touched the pillow. I couldn't follow her immediately thanks to the constant hustle and bustle in my mind. Mama used to say sleeplessness is the curse of a guilty mind—little did she nor I know then how true those words were.

Sitting up I blow out the candle on another day and listen to Martha's gentle snoring in the darkness.

I wonder what secrets this house still has to reveal to me.

And if they will all turn out to be so tragic.

Chapter 11

"You can't just go home, Serena, it will seem terribly rude," papa says.

He scowls at me. Moira is still seated in the pew, her dress of green brocade not appropriate for the warm season in my opinion, but it will have been expensive. She's always keen to display their wealth.

I'm cornered, stuck firmly between a rock and a hard place. If I stay or if I go there will be no hope of finding peace, but right at this moment the latter seems the best of poor options.

I was foolish enough to think I could do it. I thought I could stand and watch the nuptials of my former love and his cold little bride. Two days have passed, and my anger has given me a resolve at least.

I have had a lucky escape. Dicken has chosen his path and he's now welcome to grow old with discontentment and regret. No amount of money in the world will salve those wounds.

"I've been unwell, papa, and I must go home before I make a show of myself. Surely this would be worse."

I catch a disapproving tut from Moira and they exchange disparaging looks.

"Let her go," she whispers to papa, "she will only spoil the day for us if she stays."

I close my eyes to shut out her face, her voice. Pretence is a kind of purgatory and I've had too much of it of late.

When I helped Rowena into her bridesmaid dress this morning, I sowed the seed I might not be over my chill.

"To be honest, Mama and I were saying only yesterday you still look a little peaky and not yourself."

She twirled from the mirror to look at me, so I had to turn my head from her scrutiny.

"Enough about me," I said, "you will have a lovely day with Timothy."

Timothy is best man and she chief bridesmaid, so he and Rowena will be sitting together at the top table for the wedding breakfast. She told me they have shared a few stolen kisses over the last few weeks on his frequent visits to Wentworth. All very chaste and uncomplicated and for a moment I envied her. She was hoping to introduce me to a friend of his, also a guest, but really, truly I cannot think of anything I would like less.

Papa now turns his attention from Moira to me. I can't hear his sigh, but I can see it; he too is as stuck as I am for different reasons. He reaches for his wallet from the inside pocket of his grey morning suit and presses some money into my palm.

"Take a carriage home then if you really can't stay. They queue just over the bridge," he says.

Kissing him quickly on his cheek I snatch the money like a starving beggar. Hurrying now down the side of the Minster, I pass the murmuring guests fidgeting in their seats. I must get away before Dicken arrives.

Outside a fine drizzle has people jostling with umbrellas or sheltering under the sacred oak tree. I spot Rowena deep in conversation with Anabelle's sister, waiting for the arrival of the groom and then the bride. I'm thankful for her distracting my friend.

More guests line the precinct, their eyes following me as much as the scent of their fancy perfumes and pomades as I almost scurry down the cobbled street. I'm unable to stop myself breaking into a trot though I know this is attracting more attention.

As I turn the corner, my relief is shattered as I see the wedding cab approaching, four gleaming white horses, bedecked in French blue plumes and white ribbon. Passers-by wave in celebration, gentlemen removing their hats.

As the carriage passes me, I look through the window to see Dicken chatting to Timothy. I turn quickly away but not before I'm forced to acknowledge how handsome he looks in his morning suit. He seems relaxed, ready to start his new life like any other groom-to-be this Saturday.

Timothy spots me. He stops talking and nudges Dicken, who looks over his shoulder and our eyes lock. He leans out of the window to say something but my trot has increased to a run and I disappear from view. I lean against the wall of an apothecary, my breathing laboured, the rain soaking my dress and hair. I'm thankful this street is quieter.

Will Dicken be glad I wonder. Will he be relieved he doesn't have to pretend his secret isn't in the vicinity the whole day, marring what should be the happiest day of his life?

Oh, I should think so.

*

I hear the clatter of hooves as the horse's approach in the driveway, my hand instinctively resting on my stomach. This is something I've taken to doing. The idea of being pregnant is less in my thoughts and I'm becoming more attuned by the day of the reality of a baby growing inside me. I seem to be developing the protective instinct of a mother.

The horses signal papa and Moira's homecoming. I blow out unsteadily attempting to settle my nerves.

They both stayed at the best hotel in York last night after the wedding. Whilst they were enjoying themselves at Dicken's wedding blissfully unaware, I'd spent yesterday rehearsing how to break the news to them. The news that will change our lives irrevocably, the news that will bring shame on our family.

Wringing my hands, I sit then stand then sit again to await their entrance to the parlour.

"We'll have tea if you could arrange it, please, Milner," papa instructs our butler as he relieves them of their coats. He enquires if they had a pleasant time at the wedding.

"Yes, it was a splendid day, the Minster was an impressive setting. It was only a pity Miss Serena couldn't stay and enjoy it. Where is she by the way?"

"You'll find her in the parlour, sir. Tea will be served in five minutes," he says.

Moira opens the door and pretends she hasn't seen me until papa arrives. She sits by the window in her usual chair, a chair which once belonged to mama though I always try hard not to think about this.

"So, you're feeling better then. I must say it was very uncomfortable explaining your absence away all day to the guests and especially to the Carter-Knowles's as you can imagine. Rowena was most concerned."

I know she would say more on the subject if papa wasn't home but today, she must check her tongue.

Moira has cultivated the way she speaks over time. She's from a working-class background, and her accent was strong, but she tries hard to enunciate her words making her sound affected. I doubt she will convince anybody. Her hair is mousy, and she wears it always in a bun with perfectly coiffed curls about her ears. She is quite attractive but it's difficult to see past the special expression she saves for me. I think she will have had plenty of attention in her youth, and middle age will be more difficult for her because of it. Papa took her from a cashier at the bank to the life of luxury she now seems to take for granted. They bicker constantly but I've come to realise papa would rather be in a relationship with anyone who would have him than be alone. I think of Rowena's comment about Anabelle, perhaps he's not unusual. Perhaps true love is just too much to ask.

Papa looks pleased to see me as he settles himself, enquiring if I'm feeling more myself. As I nod and we share a smile, I think of my dearest wish which would be for us to live just he and I.

Moira sits staring into the fire as papa tells me about the food and wine served at the wedding and how much he thinks it will have cost. An obscene amount is his considered opinion. Money is always a point of discussion I realise, but I have never once heard Rowena's family speak of it.

That is until the day Dicken let the side down abysmally.

I must wait for tea to arrive to avoid further interruptions. I'd much prefer not to have any distractions when I tell them the news. The words are lying in wait at the back of my throat ready to burst out.

As soon as Milner leaves the room, I close my eyes briefly almost as though I'm in prayer.

"Papa, I must speak to you and Moira about something," I say, "Something that … something I'm not very proud of."

Both their faces fly in my direction, their expressions alert and perplexed at the same time. The clock on the mantlepiece is ticking loudly in the silence as we look at each other.

Moira's eyes widen with a dawning, the penny dropping rather quickly for her. It was as though she was expecting it to happen, waiting for it almost. A smug smile appears but it really doesn't bother me one jot. Sitting opposite, papa's mouth in contrast is pinched tightly, his brows pulling together. He has no idea.

"Ah, I see," she says, looking directly at me for once, "so, now you have fallen into the mire you expect your father and I to pull you out, I imagine."

I look at papa, who remains silent. He still has no idea what is happening.

"Who pray tell is the father?"

Papa's head swivels between both of us, a shadow passing his face. He swallows manically, at a loss for words for a long moment.

"Serena! How could you?" he almost whispers.

His cheeks grow so red I'm alarmed as he looks as though he might have a heart attack. I put a palm to my forehead, agitation meaning I'm unable to stay in my seat any longer. Walking across the rug I stand and stare through the window seeing nothing.

Papa strides over to pull me roughly by the shoulder so I almost fall but he doesn't notice or care.

"Well? Out with it! Who is he, he must be held to account and do the right thing."

He glowers at me, waiting for my answer. I can't tell him. How can I tell him when it will cause so much damage to not one but two families? Two families who have strong business connections at that.

As papa fumes and glowers, Moira seizes her moment, and in a frighteningly measured tone says, "It gives me no pleasure to say this Serena, but if you won't tell us, we will have no alternative but to ask you to leave. The honour and reputation of the family demands it. You cannot ask your father to bear such shame."

I'd almost forgotten Moira was there. She knows she holds all the cards suddenly, and she's apparently skilled in playing them.

I turn to Papa hoping beyond hope for some vestige of support but his gaze is fixed and he looks very close to losing control. I back away slowly to stand at the rear of the settee, using it as a barrier between us. My next admission will only fan the flames I know, but I have no option but to say it.

"Papa, I beg of you, I cannot disclose the name of the man in question. I wish I could, believe me, but it will cause more harm than good."

Narrowing his eyes his expression is menacing. I now have more than a sense of foreboding; cold fear gets a grip of me.

"Cannot or will not disclose it?" he asks skirting slowly around the settee as though stalking his prey.

His lower lip curls over his teeth, a look in his eye letting me know I'm in danger. My mind goes quickly to my baby.

"Is it that boy, is it Dicken Carter-Knowles; is it? Tell me… now!"

I jump at his bellowed final word then back away when he lunges toward me. As his hand raises, I turn to pick up my skirts. I must get out of here, I must. My father has never before raised a hand to me, and I now no longer only have myself to protect.

Passing a bewildered Milner in the hallway I only know I must run as far and as wide as I can to safety. I must flee with only the clothes on my back to my name.

I am alone and there is suddenly nothing and nobody for me to stay for in this house which was once my dear home.

Chapter 12

"Leave that now," Mr Mallerby says, "I can't bear to watch you struggling in your … condition. I think Martha may need to take over fire duties for the time being, but I'm perfectly capable of doing it for tonight."

He's referring to the condition which can no longer be disguised under layered skirts and coats even if I wanted to. Until the last two weeks I have found it quite easy to work as normal. Now Martha is to be swamped with more duties until I'm able to help again. I'm feeling more useless by the day.

He must have seen something in my face, saying now, "Perhaps you could do an exchange for a job with less exertion. It won't be forever."

I manage to raise a small smile somehow wishing to placate him. He thoughtfulness touches me.

"Yes, you're right, sir, I've become a little ungainly of late. I'll be glad when the baby is here now."

"You should rest whilst you have the chance. From the little I know about new-born babies they are not conducive to resting."

He laughs kindly and his generally sombre looking face suddenly has a softness about it taking me by surprise. I think of his wife and what happened to them. How painful it must be to think you are to become a parent only to have your hopes and dreams dashed. I will be a reminder to him of those times and this is not sitting well with me.

The room is snug. The fire's now roaring with the spruce tree stretching to the tall ceiling lit with candles.

There's one in here and one in the wide hallway and they're a pleasure to see on a cold winter's night.

My period of confinement is due to start on the last day of the year, some ten days from now and Martha has everything in hand. On Mr Mallerby's instruction, our rooms have been freshly painted along with the crib. My throat caught when she told me but as far as he's aware he assumes I know nothing of his past.

Martha said he was insistent I have everything I need including a perambulator which is on order from Cuthbert's in Malton. She won't hear of it being in the house before the baby is born due to her superstitions; and she has many. The crib too is under cover in the carpenter's workshop until the day the baby arrives and not a moment sooner. I also wouldn't want to tempt fate.

"At least we don't have a troop of guests staying for the festive season," Mr Mallerby says now, "I couldn't think of anything worse than Christmas with hordes of people you don't see the rest of the year. There's a reason for this so why should Christmas be different I wonder."

The thought of him alone on Christmas Day upsets me a little but Martha assures me he's never been one for company at the best of times.

"Do you have family, Renee; a mother perhaps to visit?"

He looks now as though he could cut out his own tongue, realising I wouldn't be in my current position if I had any family worth their salt.

"I'm afraid my mother passed away three years ago when I was just eighteen. My father remarried but my stepmother wasn't cast of the same mould as my mother shall we say."

In wanting to alleviate his discomfort I've disclosed too much.

"Ah, you must miss your mother terribly, particularly at the moment," he says quietly looking into the fire, "My wife saw a great deal of her mother as most women tend to."

I blink away my tears, turning quickly to grab a yule log from the stack on the hearth. The fire doesn't need tending but I must have something to do.

A terrible twinge appears suddenly, and I take a sharp intake of breath, grabbing my stomach. The pain is increasing so rapidly I would like to yell out. Instead, I drop back into the ladies' chair breathing heavily and paying little heed to politeness.

Mr Mallerby strides across the room, bending at the knee so our eyes are level.

"What is it?" he asks, his voice almost shrill, "Surely the baby isn't coming yet, it's far too early."

My face contorts into a grimace, making him run to pull the cord for Mr Slater. Returning quickly to my side he hesitates before putting his hand over mine. The warmth sinks into me making me think of the day I wore his coat. The comfort doesn't last long before another pain takes hold of me.

Martha knocks then bustles into the room, her eyebrows lifting at the extraordinary scene in the front parlour. She recovers quickly and as if a switch has been flicked, she sets the wheels in motion for her well-oiled plan. I have never been more thankful for a plan.

She hoists me to my feet, and I let out the howl which has been threatening to appear. She lets go of my arm quickly, so I drop back down in the chair, landing like a sack of potatoes. I wish we were alone.

"Mr Slater has retired for the night, sir," Martha says, stroking my hair, "I'll go rouse him and ask him to run for Dr Cheadle. I won't be a moment."

Our panic-stricken expressions follow her as she hurries out of the room.

"Come… Renee, let's get you to the settee at least so you will be more comfortable. Take my arm and I'll help you."

I do as he asks, holding onto his forearm. I feel the fine silk of his housecoat and for a moment I think of papa. I want to cry, then I'm strangely grateful for the distraction of another flood of pain as I lie curled on my side to try and ease it.

Crouching again he strokes my hand seeming remarkably calm despite being in unfamiliar territory.

"Hold on, Dr Cheadle won't be long," his soft voice is soothing.

My hands clawing a cushion, I hear Martha's voice.

"We must try to get her upstairs if you please, sir."

"No, please, I can't move, leave me be," I moan, pain overriding any care of who is in the room.

"Hush now, I'll go upstairs out of the way, I'm sure Wainwright will be more help than I. You can stay right where you," he tells me.

He gives my hand a final pat then rises to his full height to head off.

"Thank you kindly, sir," Martha says on my behalf.

I hear the front doorbell and the parlour door opening. Dr Cheadle's brusque no-nonsense tone immediately commands Martha to gather a list of essentials from the kitchen. He bends down to tend to me, the cold evening air still clinging to his coat before he takes it off.

"I've arrived in the nick of time by the look of it," he says rolling up his sleeves, and oh, how right he turned out to be.

Baby Hannah Marie Wilton-Robbins or Hannah Marie Robson as she will be known to the world, is born some five minutes later at thirty-seven minutes past ten on the twentieth day of December 1902. It is a Tuesday.

"There now, you were quite the model patient, Renee," Dr Cheadle says handing my new daughter to Martha.

Martha's face is wet with perspiration and tears, and I know I would never have managed the birth without her. Our bond is cemented.

I watch through teary eyes as she wraps baby Hannah snugly in a blanket so only her tiny head can be seen. Then on her knees, Martha places my daughter in my arms.

I stare at my baby's shock of auburn hair much like my own and my mother's. I've named her after my mother and the name suits her perfectly. I draw my forefinger over her features, no different I'm sure to any other new mother in the world. I'm drowning in love and fascination of a tiny, new life.

Martha takes her from me so Dr Cheadle can finish my care. I'm almost itching to have my daughter back in my arms, but I must be patient.

"I'll be on my way now," the doctor says eventually, pulling on his coat, "but I shall call tomorrow to check all is well."

Martha gets up from her knees to see him to the door.

"Oh, I beg your pardon, sir, I didn't see you there," Martha says when she opens it, her voice high pitched with alarm.

"I was waiting in the dining room. Are mother and baby fit and well?" Mr Mallerby asks.

I'm horrified. So, it appears he was in earshot of the dramatic episode the whole time.

Martha assures him all is well, then he and the doctor exchange pleasantries before he leaves.

Then a very strange thought appears from nowhere, one which takes me unawares. All I can think is I would dearly love to hear Mr Mallerby's voice soothing me and the comfort of his hand on mine again.

If only for one more time.

Chapter 13

"Martha, if I don't leave my room this very day, I shall go stark staring mad!"

Hannah is lying contentedly in her crib and there's plenty I could be doing to help in the house. I'm sick of the sight of the four walls.

"Don't take it out on me, Renee, the master won't hear of it just yet. The birth may have been quick, but it was hardly straight forward."

I think of the complications which set in only hours after the birth which nearly led me to a stay in hospital if it hadn't been for the prompt action of Dr Cheadle.

"I know, Martha and I'm grateful for his benevolence, truly I am, but life must go on. I feel as though I'm imprisoned after forty-one days and nights. This is plenty long enough for recuperation surely."

"Alright, I'll ask him again when I go down after supper with Hannah."

She can't help the twitch of a small smile at my exasperation.

I've noticed Mr Mallerby has come home a little earlier since the Christmas break. At first, he enquired after our health with Martha every day, but then on Christmas Eve something odd happened: he asked if I would allow him to meet the baby.

"He was fair shy about asking, I could tell," she told me, "Would you be agreeable?"

I was surprised by the request, but I also found it endearing he should want to become acquainted with my baby when he certainly had no need to.

Martha couldn't wait to tell me what happened after Hannah's first visit downstairs.

"Well, would you believe he only had a solid silver rattle to hand when we went in? He shook it gently while I held Hannah in my arms, and he was so happy when she opened her eyes briefly. He seemed quite taken with her, but then he would be," she paused, "but now he's asked if I can take her down for a while tomorrow."

"Christmas Day?" I asked, taken aback.

Martha nodded. I shrugged wondering what harm it could do.

"I don't see why not," I said.

On Christmas morning we were all given presents. Martha told me they will have been bought and wrapped by Mr Mallerby's secretary at Millthwaite's, Miss Rutland. Martha and Mr Slater were given a scarf and I a bed jacket to keep me warm as I recovered in bed. But Hannah, she was presented with an exquisite teddy bear, the same colour as her hair and as soft as duck down. I gasped when Martha brought it back up with her. She says its imported and very expensive. We've named him Mallers as we both agreed it suited him. Was the colour match a coincidence, or had Mr Mallerby chosen the bear especially I wondered.

Only five days after the birth, I ate my beautifully presented Christmas dinner on a tray in bed and Martha sat at a little table by the fireside. Mr Mallerby consented to Mr Slater going home for once to eat with his mother. Martha asked him along to one of her little meetings with Hannah before he left, as she couldn't stand the thought of Mr Slater being alone on Christmas Day morning.

"Mr Slater was chuffed to bits," Martha said, "he told me he couldn't remember the last time he'd seen his mother on Christmas Day. He usually had to wait until Boxing Day to go home."

How happy everyone seemed with the arrangement. I tried not to think about Mr Mallerby eating alone at the long dining table.

Martha bought a tiny tree and decorated it with a handful of wooden keepsakes passed down from her grandmother, making the room look cosy and festive. It was dusk by the time we ate our meal, and she said Mr Mallerby had kept the day quietly, but he had spent nearly an hour with Hannah. It interfered with Martha's chores, but I'm sure she will have done it all with a smile on her face.

"He always asks if there's anything you need before I leave," Martha said.

"Hardly, Martha," I said, "Hannah is well provided for after you went on that spree. She has everything she needs for the winter season at least."

I felt blessed. Oddly, it was the best Christmas I'd had by a country mile since mama died.

"I saw a card arrive two days ago with what I think was the mistress's handwriting on the envelope," Martha said after our meal.

She was pouring both of us a sherry from a bottle she'd bought in the village. Purely for medicinal purposes she insisted.

"I posted a card to her from the master. After what you said about her never coming back, I decided to keep a note of her mother's address this time."

"Martha, why would you do that?" I said too loudly. Hannah stirred and I lifted her from her crib by the bed to lay her at my breast.

"What do you mean? That's nothing," Martha protested, "my mother would have steamed the letters open—God rest her soul—she always said forewarned is forearmed in life."

Though I was shocked I couldn't help but smile at her honesty. Her forthright ways are my most favourite thing about Martha. I've been glad of them many a time.

She cleared her throat.

"What was your mother like, Little Robin?"

I could tell she'd been dying to ask the question; a second glass of sherry had loosened her tongue.

I took a deep breath. Christmas night was the perfect time to tell her everything she wished to know about my mother. It was the right time.

"Not surprisingly, Martha I've been thinking about my mother a lot since Hannah was born. She was a true lady, even when riled, which was rare but then, my oh my, she was a sight to behold. My father once spoke out of turn I remember, and she showed him the error of his ways without even raising her voice. They were in love, I could sense it looking back, but this isn't something you consider when you're a child. When you become an adult, you understand."

I pressed my lips together to stop them from trembling, finding it difficult to go on.

"She wasn't overly demonstrative, but she showed affection in subtle ways: gentle kisses goodnight, light touches of her hand on mine, asking me how I was feeling. I told her everything, Martha; everything."

My voice cracked and I looked down at my own daughter. I prayed in that moment I will be half the mother she was.

"She sounds like a real queen. I wish I could have met her," Martha said with a sad smile.

I pictured Martha and my mother together, both from very different backgrounds but cut from the same cloth. Both ladies, both good, kind women.

I thought how Martha had been sent to fill a void in my heart, and a tear slid down my cheek.

"She would have loved you as much as I do, Martha, I'm certain of it."

My friend's face glowed, and not only from the effects of the fire and the sherry, I thought. I had never spoken a truer word in my life.

Chapter 14

What has happened between Mr Mallerby and his wife; why will she never come home? I can't help asking myself the questions regularly.

Mr Mallerby still drags a sense of sadness around with him like a sack. My mother would have called it melancholia. He is melancholic.

Hannah seems to be the only one who can relieve it, but even then, only temporarily.

If he knows where his wife is then why doesn't he visit or bring her home? Surely the exchange of Christmas cards means they still have feelings for each other. Another letter arrived only today Martha reliably informed me.

He has a bright smile on his face as he turns to me, and I'm thrown by the sincerity of it. How handsome he is, the life in his features making the years drop away.

"I can't believe she's sitting up by herself already. My, what a clever girl you are," he says.

He strokes Hannah's head gently as she sits with toys strewn around her feet on the fireside rug. She's wearing her navy blue and white sailor dress with a red bow at the collar which Mr Mallerby was kind enough to buy.

I was decidedly awkward in the beginning during these peculiar play sessions, but now I find them almost companiable.

He has done so much for me; too much when you consider I am a servant. Had he not been such a solitary figure I think it would have set tongues wagging in the district. As it is, Slater and the other staff are very loyal to Mr Mallerby and don't talk idly to others about the goings on at the hall. He is a kind and fair master and deserves no less, I think.

As Hannah plays innocently, I wonder if I look as sad as he. We've both loved and lost and perhaps this is impossible to hide however hard we try.

Suddenly he turns to me and breaks the silence.

"Have you given any more thought to my offer Renee…about securing a nanny for Hannah."

"I can't help but think a nanny is far too much of an imposition, not to mention highly irregular for a man in your position," I say, sensing how dismissive I sound to such a generous gift. I am feeling far from dismissive.

He sits back in his chair and rolls his eyes.

"Please, I've no time for convention if this is what's bothering you. I know there are those at Millthwaite's who think me a bit odd, but this is of no concern to me. Hannah is a part of this household and if you are to stay here and fulfil your duties then we must see that she is properly looked after. So, if you would like a nanny, I can't see any reason why you shouldn't have one."

I manage to stop myself smiling at his indignant tone and at the fact he clearly doesn't want us to leave. I swell with happiness.

"Once again, I thank you for your generosity, I can assure you that there'll be no backsliding in my work sir. Martha and I manage very well between us, and Mr Slater often sits with Hannah if we're hanging washing or pulling vegetables from the garden. I think he quite likes her on the quiet."

"I'm certain he does," he pauses, his eyes twinkling, "perhaps there's someone else in the house he quite likes too."

My cheeks grow hot at the note of playfulness in his voice. It's so unlike him.

"I wouldn't know about such things. I find him to be very considerate and I often think he's a person who is better for knowing. I've certainly come to see him as a friend over the last few months."

This is the first time we've ever spoken to each other in such a way and I need to be careful that Renee's mask doesn't slip again. I pile Hannah's building blocks as a distraction then she knocks them over with a delighted look on her face.

I might be imagining it, but I can feel his eyes burning into the top of my lowered head.

This night has taken an unexpected and decidedly unsettling turn.

*

Two days later, Hannah is tucked up in her crib as I do my final round of the rooms for the evening. Martha and Mr Slater have retired to bed, and I want to stoke the fires and check everything is in order before I head upstairs. This is my usual routine.

I knock once, then again on the parlour door before I enter the room. I thought I would be alone, so I'm alarmed when I see Mr Mallerby sitting in his chair with a letter in his hand. It must be the letter from his wife; it can't surely be any other though I wouldn't recognise the handwriting.

"I'm sorry, sir, I knocked twice and thought you would be in your study."

His eyes are glazed as he looks up at me. Here's staring right through me and I wonder whether I should leave the room. But then as he continues to stare at me, my heart begins to pound wondering if he's had bad news.

I clear my throat.

"Are you unwell, Mr Mallerby?" I ask.

His Adam's apple bobs up and down his throat, but the silence still hangs between us. He looks as though he's about to lose control.

"How to answer that, Renee," he says, forlornly, "I don't know what to do, I really and truly do not know what to do."

The pain in his voice cuts me. I close the door quietly to lean against it.

"You have helped me so much, sir. If there is anything I can do to help you now, you must tell me."

His eyes finally focus on me, and I catch my breath. I've never seen such raw emotion in anyone's eyes before. I have no idea how to react to it.

"Can you keep a secret?" he asks.

Oh, if only you knew, I think.

"Yes, of course."

He puts the letter to one side but doesn't look at me.

"My wife isn't visiting her sick mother. This is what I've told people at home and at work, but it's a lie."

Now, finally the mystery may be revealed; the intrigue has hounded my thoughts for too long.

"To be honest sir, I had guessed as much," I say.

Sighing, he nods toward the settee for me to sit down.

"How did you know?" he asks flatly.

I'm not sure how much I should tell him, so I don't give too much away.

"It was just a feeling, perhaps an instinct at first," I say, "but then if you recall, on the day you discovered I was with child, you told me she would never return . I found it a very peculiar thing to say."

"Of course, I remember disclosing that now. It was such a momentous day which seems like another life ago." He pauses, his eyes far away as though he's in a state of reflection.

"You know, I love having a baby in the house."

I open and close my mouth; what can I say to such a candid statement? I decide to stare at the fire rather than say the wrong thing.

"My wife was a difficult woman, but even so I cared deeply for her. Her family is wealthy, her father a lord, and we met at a summer ball in Harrogate which I wasn't keen to attend. I detest formality the same now as I did then. She was unlike any woman I had ever met before; lively, exciting even and she made me feel as though I was the only person at the ball. Within six months I had proposed, and she had accepted. I think now I proposed so quickly because I was worried that she might tire of me and disappear if I didn't.

He takes a sip of brandy, making me wonder if he's had more than he should to be speaking to me in this way.

"Clearly, we weren't blessed with a family, and this created a void between us. When we should have clung together, it sadly drew us apart … or at least it drew her apart from me."

The candle on the chairside table has burnt down to nothing and his face in profile is glowing in the firelight. This man is in so much turmoil, I think. His wife has left him to flounder.

Taking leave of my senses but following my instincts, I lean over and place my hand on his. He turns his palm upwards to grasp it.

"You are such a beautiful woman, Renee, it makes me sad to think of you widowed and alone so young, your husband never being able to see his wonderful little daughter."

I hold my breath.

If I don't, I risk a strangled cry escaping me.

Shame on you, Serena, I think. Shame on you that you would deceive this wonderful, tortured soul.

Chapter 15

A pounding on the door has Mr Slater up and running from the table.

The hammering is relentless and then, as I run up the cellar steps, I hear voices. I'm closely followed by Martha, her face hanging with terrified look. Neither of us speak a word as we take the steps together quickly, paying little heed to our safety. I already feel sick.

One minute we were having our cocoa and talking of Hannah's latest antics, the next this.

"I don't want to wait until the morning. I want to speak to her now and I demand you fetch her this instant if you know what's good for you."

My heart plummets as I recognise the voice. It's the voice of Dicken Carter-Knowles.

Martha and I emerge into the dimly lit hall to stand at the side of Mr Slater who for once is struggling to keep his composure. So, this is it, my life as I know it is over.

"Ah, there she is. Serena, how perfectly lovely to see you after all this time. You took some finding, I must say," he says, pushing Mr Slater to one side.

Mr Slater stumbles but I manage to catch him before he falls then I step in front of him, holding my palms up to stop Dicken from coming any further into the hall.

"Dicken, have you been drinking? I will speak to you tomorrow if you don't mind, now is not the time nor the place," I say.

"Now is not the time nor the place," he mimics in a whiny voice.

We stand staring at each other, eyes glowering.

"May I suggest you do yourself a favour sir and leave my premises before I'm forced to eject you myself."

The booming voice of Mr Mallerby startles me as I whip around to see him storming down the hallway toward us.

He guides me around the back of him to stand between Dicken and me.

"And just who the hell are you?" Dicken barks sarcastically.

"I am Dawson Mallerby, though this is no business of yours. This is my house, and I will thank you for leaving it immediately."

Dicken lifts his chin and plants his feet, the slight sway of his body spoiling the effect.

"I don't care who you are. I'm here to see Serena and my child and you will not stand in my way."

I look at Martha over my shoulder and see her expression change as she realises now who we're dealing with. I stand in the midst of the commotion, wondering how Dicken has managed to find me.

"There is no-one here by that name. It would appear you have made a mistake so I will ask you only once more to leave."

Mr Mallerby takes a step forward to stand over Dicken. He is taller and broader his face set like stone.

"Shall we?" he says gesturing to the door. Dicken moves backward but before Mr Mallerby can close the door, he puts his foot in the way.

"This woman is here under false pretences. It would be in your best interests to throw her out onto the street where she came from."

Mr Mallerby takes a step forward and Dicken instinctively takes a step backwards.

"Be gone and if I see you on my property again, I shall have no hesitation in calling the constable."

His voice is level but there's no mistaking the menacing tone. Dicken, just go home, I think.

His eyes on fire Dicken clenches and unclenches his hand but Mr Mallerby only stares at him unflinching.

Beaten, Dicken turns on his heel and storms down the stone steps. Though he's admitting defeat for now, I doubt it will be for long. I'm ashamed of him and his behaviour tonight and he's not even mine to feel ashamed of.

I race outside, instantly cooled by the summer rain. I must know where Dicken is heading and satisfy myself that he's left the premises. At the end of the drive, I see him climb into his carriage, the horses soon galloping away from the village. I stand still, watching until he disappears into the darkness.

Too shaken to weep, if it wasn't for Hannah sleeping upstairs, I would carry on walking in the rain never to return to Mallerby Hall. The disgrace is too much to face.

But face it I must.

By the time I return to the house everyone has disbanded, not a soul in sight. Now isn't the time for the inquest. So, I must go to bed and fret about seeing Mr Mallerby and Mr Slater in the morning. The night stretches ahead like the darkest tunnel.

I lock the door and bolt it leaning my head against the glass.

"Renee, if that is indeed your name, I would be grateful if you could join me a moment before you retire."

The coldness of Mr Mallerby's tone chills me as I turn from the door. He's waiting in the parlour out of sight for now.

Dropping my head back I cross the threshold to stand with my hands knotted in front of me waiting to be chastised.

"Close the door behind you," he says.

I think of our tender moment only days ago. How he offloaded all his troubles, how we almost kissed. A log shifted on the fire and startled us, bringing us to our senses so a kiss never happened. But for a log it would have happened I somehow know it.

He stands at the fireplace gesturing with his hand for me to sit on the settee. I perch in the exact same spot as before.

But since that night everything has changed and not for the better.

"I'm waiting for an explanation though I can hazard a guess what it might be."

Where to begin. How to begin but now as I speak the first word the rest come gushing out.

"Your suspicions are correct. I'm ashamed to admit it, sir, but they are and I'm terribly sorry for bringing this to your doorstep. I am here under false pretences. I ran away from home after my father and stepmother discovered I was pregnant. I had nowhere to go, so I slept in an outhouse of the factory until … until I was discovered."

"I see," he says, "so if you're not Renee, then who are you?"

I raise my eyes and take a deep breath. I know I owe this man the truth.

"Serena Wilton-Robbins."

He takes a step back his mouth open. Whatever he was expecting, it wasn't that.

"The daughter of Charles Wilton-Robbins? It cannot be surely; I do business with your father's bank!"

His voice is raised without a thought for the rest of the household.

Renee Robson who has been my alter ego all these months has suddenly evaporated into thin air, and I miss her already.

"I truly didn't want to deceive you, but you must understand I was in dire straits. I was destitute and desperate, there was Hannah to think of and then Martha offered me a way out." I gasp, suddenly realising the danger I've brought to Martha's door, "Please don't reproach her, she's the dearest person I've ever met, and I hate to think she might be in trouble because of me, because she showed kindness to a person in distress."

He rakes a hand through his hair then stares at me so long I must look away.

"Martha is not in trouble. She's just the same as her mother was, always drawn to a lame duck. Before she died her mother was a huge support to my wife, and I think our situation went from bad to worse afterwards."

His head leans as he continues to stare at me.

"I take it that awful man is the father?" he asks.

Awful is the word. Absence did not make my heart grow fonder in this instance.

"Yes, his name is Dicken Carter-Knowles. He's the brother of my former best friend, I stayed with them regularly after my mother's death and we became…close," I say, almost wincing at how I could ever have felt anything for the man who burst in and destroyed our happy lives here.

Mr Mallerby looks shaken by the turn of events, and I'm at the root of it.

"You should have told me; I would have understood. I would have understood because you were just a child, a lonely, grieving child who he took advantage of. I can picture it.

I want to believe what he's saying, this would ease my guilt. Yet I know Dicken didn't take advantage of me. I gave myself to him willingly.

"I don't believe that was the case," I say, my voice small.

I cannot deceive this man any longer.

"I'm sure he pursued you, made you believe you would have a future together; I see the kind of man he is. I can see right through him."

I don't want to hear it.

"Please don't be kind to me, I… I can't bear it."

Reaching for a handkerchief I dab my eyes and try to strangle a sob. When I fail, he leans over to touch my arm, such a featherlight touch which brings me the same solace it did on the night Hannah was born. The gap between our seats is oceanwide but our eyes lock just long enough to bridge it.

His eyes are blazing with passion as he clasps my hands between his like he's holding a small, fragile bird, afraid it's wings might break at his touch.

"Oh Renee, Serena; I don't care who you are or who you were. I only know that from the very first moment I saw you, something stirred deep within me and now I cannot stop thinking about you. Not for one second. Can you not see it?"

He drops to his knee and I know he's going to kiss me; I want him to and when our lips meet, I fall into the sensation, I drown in it.

Our kissing becomes more fervent, so fervent it stirs something within me now. I feel him lift my skirts, his hands seeking what he's so desperate to find. When he touches what he wants so badly he groans, and I like the sound of it.

He stands to untie his house robe, then unbutton his shirt to display a chest strewn with dark hairs trailing to a taut stomach belying his years. I don't care about those years; I only want to feel his body close to me. When I take it, he drops his head back savouring the pleasure of it.

"If you want me to stop, say it now," he says.

"I don't want you to stop," I whisper.

He gently pushes me back to lay on the cushions as he grapples through my skirts with exasperation. I'm so pleased when he finally finds what he's seeking and slides himself inside me. We both burn with yearning and longing, yet for me there's something more.

Thrusting, panting together the emotion builds so slowly, so hauntingly, I place my hand on my mouth to stop from crying out. This may as well be my first time of loving because of the way my heart pours into his as though molten rock to a mould, joined and set for all time.

As he falls onto my chest, he breathes heavily into my unruly curls which have fallen from their braid, and I run my fingers through the waves of his hair. I've wanted to do this since the first time I saw him, I realise.

"What have we done?" I ask rhetorically, my tone light, so glad that we did it.

He lifts his head and smiles. I smile back but then my throat tightens as I see the sadness, the one which always sits just behind his eyes, it still remains.

I would like to tell him that I love him, but I can't. His look of sorrow stops me from saying aloud the words, yet only seconds ago they were poised to fire from my heart.

So, I swallow them quickly. They will have to stay locked away for now, perhaps forever.

I do love this man I think, as his thumb caresses my shoulder, his breathing slowing.

But I know that whatever this man feels for me, he is still in love with his wife, whatever she has done, and whether she reciprocates his love … or not.

Chapter 16

Martha rummages in the top drawer of the kitchen dresser searching for a very particular recipe book. She slides a piece of paper from inside the back cover pulling her bottom lip as she studies the words intently.

"The Beeches, Clover Crescent, Harrogate - number sixteen by the look of it," she tells me smoothing the paper with her knotted fingers.

Harrogate – now there's a place I haven't been to in many a year. Not since one Christmas when we stayed at the Black Swan and papa took the waters. Mama and I had afternoon tea at Harriet's and went shopping for our gifts at Dalton & Browns. I didn't have a care in the world that festive weekend though how could I know it then?

I'm certain this trip will turn out to be far less leisurely and far less decadent.

"And you're sure you'll manage if I leave Hannah with you? I'll send you a telegram if I'm waylaid, but I can't do what I must with her in tow."

"I know, it's better she stays here. I'll tell the master you've gone to straighten out all the nasty business with Mr Dicken. Mr Slater will be more than happy to lend a hand; you know he's smitten. In fact, our little Miss Hannah has both the men in the household wrapped around her tiny finger."

"What would I do without you?"

I draw my friend into my arms, overcome with gratitude. As she clings to me, she whispers, "Go do what you must, my Little Robin then hurry home," her eyes roam my face, "I have some money put by if you think you might need it."

I hold fast to her shoulders extending my thanks but reassure her I've managed to save quite a sum having all our needs more than taken care of by Mr Mallerby.

I'm still unable to call him Dawson though he considers this odd. Dawson Mallerby—such a distinctive, refined name, Dawson being his mother's maiden name. Although we're far more comfortable with one another, lovemaking was a one-off occurrence. It was a moment of weakness. It changed me, and my affection for him grows daily but I can only keep my secret close.

Life will change again if my plan works and for his sake, I hope that it does.

"Just don't call me sir is all I ask, Serena. This would be far too peculiar under the circumstances."

We laughed together then, but I must resign myself to the one-sided situation. If only I could stand beside him as his equal, his wife and not his lover. Sadly, I'm all too aware I'm not the keeper of his heart.

"I've mended and laundered my dress for the journey." I tell Martha, "To think how much has happened since I ran from the house wearing it that day."

I drop my arms and look at the floor, suddenly humbled.

"Do you think less of me, now you know the full story?" I ask her.

She refills our cups with tea from the teapot, which is too strong for my taste, but I could never tell her.

"No, lass; people in glass houses would do well not to throw stones, most of us have done things we're

93

not proud of. I know I can trust you when I tell you my father had a criminal record."

I stare at her aghast.

"What did he do?"

"He was jailed for brawling before he met my mother. Then when he came here, he became a pillar of the community working at the clog factory before he died. After that we moved in here and the rest is history. I barely remember him to be honest, but I do know he made a success of his life after falling off the tracks for a while."

"Ah, well, there's hope for me yet then," I say.

She smiles as we clink our teacups together in a toast.

"Get away with you, you're no criminal unless you count stealing my heart. Now, off you go and get ready for your big trip."

I check the time on the clock perched on the dresser. Just after twelve—the train is due at ten minutes past one and I've still so much to do. I hurry upstairs to change into my best clothes, what I now see as a costume. I'm no longer the entitled lady I once was, but I must play the part if I'm to succeed in my mission.

The travel bag I bought especially for the journey in one hand, I stroke Hannah's curls with the other and watch her sleeping, though I've barely time for this. Am I doing the right thing for us, little one? I have no way of knowing, only time will tell, but I know I will not rest unless I try.

Mr Slater is waiting at the bottom of the stairs for me. We've never spoken of the night Dicken descended on the house. Thankfully, he hasn't returned, though I've been living in fear that he might, and this is the last thought I have before I go to sleep and the first when I wake up. As a father he has a rightful claim on his daughter if he chose to exercise it and his circumstances are far better than my own. Perhaps Rowena has reasoned with him. In their privileged world he has so much to lose should an illegitimate child be discovered. The irony isn't lost on me that I was once part of that world; a place where love is far less important than losing face.

"May I carry your bag to the station, Mrs Robson?" Mr Slater asks. Though we haven't spoken of *the* situation he has suddenly started referring to me more formally as if I have a higher station in life. I haven't, not really but it must be very confusing for the poor man.

"How kind of you, Mr Slater but I couldn't possibly encroach on your valuable time."

"Well then, I bid you farewell and wish you a pleasant journey," he says turning to go down the hallway.

I watch him leave. What a good man he is, I think, and he dearly loves my daughter. If only I could love him our future would be secure. Is love too much to ask I wonder yet again. My expectations may be set too high when I can ill afford the luxury.

As I go down the drive I turn and raise my hand to Martha who stands waving from the dining room window. I've never been apart from her and Hannah before. Closing the gate, I decide it best not to dwell on such things.

The short journey to Hebden Bridge train station is quiet and I don't come across another soul on the deserted streets. The air is crisp, the smell of the home fires making me homesick already. I could turn back and resume my day as though nothing had happened. It's tempting but I know I shall never find peace if I do.

I purchase a ticket at the station. Under ordinary circumstances I should have a ladies' maid or a travelling companion, and the station master gave me an odd look over the top of his spectacles. He's clearly wondering why I'm alone. Clouds of smoke and screeching brakes herald the arrival of the train. A guard reaches a hand to help me aboard and loads my small bag into the overhead shelving in the compartment. I thank him with a coin but not before he too has given me another awkward look. I'm trying to settle back into the customs of my old life but I'm finding it an uncomfortable fit having been free of this world for a year.

I sit alone with my thoughts in the empty compartment which pleases me. I watch through a half misted window as town turns to countryside and back again many times. I'm now a stranger in this world but I must overcome my pensiveness if I'm to survive it.

What will Lady Barclay think of me arriving unannounced on her doorstep? I must accept it if I fall at the first hurdle and return with my tail between my legs. Yet, I must find confidence enough not to allow this to happen.

As the train slows into Leeds station, I wipe the window with my gloved hand. I hear the hissing of the steam and watch the cloud swirling around the people gathered on the platform awaiting our arrival. They will all have their own story to tell.

I close my eyes to the cold hard facts of my own story which are troubling me. I'm no longer a silly young girl, so I know I'm at risk of losing everything.

But sometimes love is in the driving seat.

Chapter 17

Having changed trains at Leeds, I arrive to the quieter and more genteel surroundings of Harrogate station some two hours later. I'm thankful for my warm coat as the weather is brisk now and I pull my warmer gloves from the depths of my bag.

I make for the line of carriages waiting in line outside and tell the driver the address as he hands me a blanket for my knees.

I've seen the tree-lined avenues around Harrogate's Stray many times and in every season. Today the trees are beginning to shed their glorious, flush of autumn colour. This is a beautiful town, though I'm now more comfortable with the cottages and terraces of my new home. The grit and grime make them less perfect and more homely.

I daydream briefly about the lives of those living in their Georgian splendour when the sound of the driver's voice brings me sharply back to reality.

"Whoa," he says as the horses slow then come to a halt, "Here we are, miss, this is the address."

He jumps down from his seat to helps me from the carriage.

"Shall I carry your bag to the door, miss?"

A polished, brass sign proclaims we are indeed at *The Beeches*.

"Thank you, but no, I shall manage," I say, handing over my fare and a little extra.

"Good day to you then, miss," he says, jumping nimbly aboard his seat and doffing his cap before setting off. I watch the carriage disappear along the avenue and think I should like to run and jump back inside. My good intentions now seem ridiculous. I can only blow out my nerves then swing open the gates and head down the gravel driveway.

Approaching the two pillars of the portico entrance, I lift my skirts to climb three stone steps. This is indeed an impressive house I think as I ring the bell but then Mr Mallerby did tell me his wife's family is one of wealth.

I tidy the wisping curls which have come free from around my ears as I wait. It's important I arrive looking pristine for my visit. A fixed smile is in place as the door opens.

"Good afternoon miss, how may I help you," the elderly butler asks.

"Good afternoon. I must apologies for arriving without an appointment however I have urgent need to speak with Lady Barclay and I would be most grateful if you would ask if she will receive me. My name is Miss Serena Wilton-Robbins, and I believe she is acquainted with my father.

He stands for too long a moment without speaking. Has he spotted something I've missed; does he know somehow that I'm an imposter who should be sent packing?

I stand firm ensuring clear eye contact.

"Well, this is most irregular miss, but if you might follow me into the hall I will enquire of her ladyship as to your request," he says, his cold eyes never leaving mine.

I step over the threshold and stand in the white marble tiled hallway, watching as he heads off down a corridor on the left to see his mistress.

A hall clock ticks the time away as I wait, almost rigid with fear. I'm far from sure I will be granted an audience. Twisting the handles of my bag between my fingers I hear the butler's footsteps increase in volume as he reappears.

"Her ladyship says she will see you, Miss Carter-Knowles. May I take your coat?" he asks me.

He returns a moment later and I set off behind him, struggling to keep up with his military pace.

The family wealth is dripping from every part of the hallway. We turn into the corridor, and I can see an array of impressive busts sitting atop polished wooden plinths, elegant wallpapers and wall rugs with intricate oriental designs. Three crystal chandeliers light the way to a reception room with a floor to ceiling arched window as its centrepiece. Wealth, yes, but taste too, I think. Money cannot buy taste as mama often said.

To the right of the window, there is a door flanked by a table and a small chair and the butler knocks lightly before entering then beckoning me to follow.

"Miss Carter-Knowles to see you, madam," he says.

This is my cue I think although I might be retracing my footsteps back to the front door quicker than I would like if I'm unable to play my part well enough.

I glance around the room my eyes settling on a small woman sitting alone by the fireside, except for a West Highland Terrier lounging on the hearth rug. There's no sign of Mrs Mallerby, and I'm suddenly unsure if her absence will help or hinder my plan.

"Good afternoon, your ladyship," I say, a little too loudly.

Confidence is not about being the loudest in the room, Serena," I can hear my mother saying. I must control my nervousness.

Lady Barclay extends her hand but says nothing. Only looks at me intently, biding her time, gathering information, I think.

"I apologise for the unscheduled interruption but hope not to take up too much of your time."

Her demeanour is neither kind nor unkind. She is scrutinising her mysterious visitor, weighing me up.

"Good afternoon indeed, Miss Carter-Knowles. I must say I am intrigued as to the nature of your visit. Please take a seat by the fire. Featherstone, be good enough to arrange refreshments."

"Very good, madam," Featherstone says leaving the room swiftly.

I think of Mr Slater with a swell of homesickness. His professional manner has more warmth to it.

The drawing room is much too large to be cosy, but the warmth of the fire is welcome on this bitterly cold afternoon. My eyes take in flights of exotic birds; guilt framed portraits, marble topped furniture. Opulent is the watchword of this house.

She lifts her hand dismissively signalling towards a chair and I know her eyes are following me as I make my way to sit down. Her greying fair hair is in a coil at the nape of her neck, her dress is duck egg blue with brown and cream lace at the neck and hemline. Mrs Mallerby has inherited her mother's colouring according to Martha's description.

"Forgive me," I say smoothing the pleats of my best dress busily, "I'm aware you are not acquainted with my father," I pause but I'm unable to look up, "this was a ruse to secure the meeting, but rest assured my visit here today is well-intended."

Her face is entirely devoid of emotion, her mouth set in a hard line, but she doesn't look in the least surprised.

"My dear, I am fully cognisant of who I am acquainted with and who I am not. However, it is fortunate for you that curiosity got the better of me this afternoon," she says, putting me firmly in my place. "So, now we have that out of the way, perhaps you could enlighten me quickly as to the purpose of your visit."

Her ice-cold tone is withering, but only briefly. I must remember my reason for being here and hold fast to my resolve.

"I am actually an acquaintance of your son-in-law and … and it is actually your daughter with whom I would like to speak if I may. I understand she's living here with you at present."

Her narrowing eyes give her an almost a feline-like expression of distrust.

"An acquaintance, you say, how tantalisingly vague. I presume he doesn't know you are here and if I know my son-in-law, I doubt he would take very kindly to it. I'm wondering what business you, a stranger as far as I am concerned, could possibly have with my daughter and her husband."

I heave a breath, licking my lips to counteract their dryness. I'm very much in need of refreshment suddenly I realise.

"My only desire is to try and help Mr Mallerby. His unhappiness is obvious though he tries to hide it."

I'm finding my voice now and before she can interrupt, I press on.

"I've no wish to waste your time so if I may speak plainly: I know your son-in-law still has feelings for your daughter."

Featherstone's knocking interrupts my flow and he emerges with a silver tray which he places on a small table between us before pouring the tea. Will she ask him to escort me from the premises now? This woman knows nothing of me and I'm entirely in her hands.

But she merely dismisses Featherstone with a cursory, "That will be all."

There is still hope for my plan after all.

"As you have spoken plainly, then so shall I. I think it odd you have come to see us today. I can see that you're not yet married and therefore have no experience in this area but let me assure you the relationship between a husband and a wife is entirely their own affair, and one that is not to be trifled with by an outsider, a third party. Even I do not involve myself in my daughter's affairs."

My face colours as I sip my tea demurely. I must think quickly how to respond without angering her further.

"I understand completely your thoughts on the matter, Lady Barclay. However, Mr Mallerby is finding life difficult shall we say, and as a friend I believe I can help. Although I know my efforts may be in vain, I know I must at least try."

She offers me the stand of dainty sandwiches and I take one, so I don't cause offence, but food is the last thing on my mind.

"It's clear that you are a lady of some breeding, and I have no doubt that you mean only to help matters, but…," she pauses to look at me, "My dear, you look terrified. I'm sure this visit will have been hard for you to make but please settle yourself, you have nothing to fear from me.

She sets her cup down on the table and her words soothe me slightly.

"However, I doubt I can help you in your endeavours. I'm afraid my daughter left this house over six months ago."

Six months ago, surely, she's mistaken! How can this be?

"Have you received no word. I hope she is quite well," I say, struggling to keep my tone level.

Dawson's wife is clearly a woman of mystery. I sense she will have kept him on his toes, yet some men like it this way or so I understand. Perhaps he would find a quiet life dull.

"Yes, she's written, and I have an address in Halifax, but I suspect you may be wasting your time and efforts."

My heart sinks. I'll need to make another journey, assuming she will disclose her daughter's whereabouts.

But I dare not ask, I can only continue nibbling at my sandwich.

"I can tell your heart is in the right place, but you should know that my daughter is a ... a troubled soul. I was unable to help her and so was her husband, and I doubt you will have better success."

I give up trying to eat my food and focus my full attention on the woman who holds my love's destiny in the palm of her hand. This is my last chance.

"All I can say is that I simply cannot sit back any longer without doing something, anything, to improve the situation at Mallerby Hall. I know Mr Mallerby would welcome his wife home with open arms should she return."

My words are full of conviction and as she stares at me in silence, I increasingly sense she believes me.

Eventually she turns to look out of the window. I follow her gaze to see dusk is descending, the rhododendrons now obscure across the lawn. I realise I must leave soon as I have yet to find rooms in the town.

"You are a determined young lady, Miss Carter-Knowles," she smiles softly at me, "and I'm still curious as to why you should take such trouble."

I feel my face warming.

"But I don't see how you could make the situation any worse, and therefore I give you my permission to find my daughter. She may not talk to you, but it seems you have a fever you must dampen, I hope Dawson appreciates how lucky he is to have such a good friend."

I play with my lace napkin, my nerves ebbing slightly.

"He has been kind to me is all. I wish him only happiness."

She nods just once, watching me with eyes full of questions.

"Well, it seems happiness has eluded them so far, but perhaps the intervention of a stranger, a neutral party at it were, may be just what they need to get them back on track. Stubbornness is a terrible affliction."

She leaves the room and returns with an address written in beautiful scribe. I study the letterheaded paper a moment then glance up and smile.

This tiny, unassuming piece of paper may well hold the key to restoring a marriage to its former glory.

Once and for all.

Chapter 18

Only hours ago, the thought of meeting Lady Barclay made my stomach swirl. How strange then she has turned out to be something of an ally.

Life is full of surprises I'm discovering but in different times I do think we could be companions, perhaps even friends. How lonely she must be having lost her husband and now her daughter has left the fold.

Lady Barclay told me she left after a quarrel. Though she didn't elaborate I sense the beautiful house she lives in has become no more than a gilded cage.

Given the hour and the fact I'm travelling alone she surprises me by asking me to stay the night. I think this far too much of an imposition though I'm grateful for her kindness and tell her so. Then yet another white lie escapes me when I say I will be staying at the *Black Swan*.

She arranges for her man to take me in her carriage to my hotel.

"I would be glad if you could update with any progress or even information, Serena," she says as I leave.

Warmed by her using my first name I smile then turn to see her sitting exactly as I found her except now even the terrier, Belfry has left to go on a walk around the grounds. She is completely alone and will be for the rest of the evening, so perhaps this is why she extended the offer to stay. It saddens me she hasn't had any contact with her daughter for six months. I could never have imagined this happening with mama under any circumstances.

The genteel Black Swan fills me with memories of a past life when I see it. They wash over me as I wait for the driver to ride off, trying to ignore the curious stare of the concierge. Last time I stayed here was with mama and papa, but my limited purse means it is now far beyond my means. I shuffle off passed the Pump Rooms and onto Ripon Road where, after a mile or so I'm able to find more modest accommodation within my budget.

I sleep soundly hoping the worst part of my expedition is now behind me. I usually dream of mama, and I do, but when I wake the distress that she is no longer here is replaced with a sense of purpose. Perhaps she is still walking beside me after all.

The journey to Halifax is pleasant, despite the gloomy weather and needing to change trains in Bradford. Arriving at the station I meet a sweet elderly gentleman in the train corridor who tells me he is taking his young grandson on his first train ride. The boy's excitement is obvious, and I find it infectious.

"I can't wait to take my baby daughter for her first ride on a train one day," I tell him.

He smiles, one hand on his cane the other holding his grandson's hand.

"We're lucky to relive our lives vicariously through our children and grandchildren are we not? Might I enquire where you are headed today, miss?" he asks me.

"I have business in Batley Street though I've never been before."

I wonder if I imagined the slight widening of his eyes.

"The address is quite central; I would be happy to give you a ride in my carriage."

His grandson tugs his grandpa's hand to pull him down the corridor.

"Thank you, sir," I say, "But I'm happy to walk if the address is nearby."

He raises an eyebrow, and his smile thins momentarily.

"As you please, miss, but it's fair walk. If you follow Winding Road and then pass the large mill on Ovenden Road, I believe it's on your left near the Baptist Church.

"Thank you, sir," I say smiling at him then his grandson.

"Farewell then, miss, and a good day to you," he says, lifting his hat.

As I walk from the station a terrible longing for Hannah winds me. She will never have a grandpa I think, nor a grandmother to pass on wisdom and make memories.

But then I have Martha who is a fine replacement. Come what may after my trip, I'd like Martha to remain a central part of our lives.

Once past the shops and grand business premises I reach the giant mill complex that is Dean Clough, one of the wonders of the age; almost a town within a town I think as I see hundreds of people scurrying busily around the site.

The road starts to rise as I pass row upon row of terraced houses. They're all the same, like soldiers lined up on parade but some are shabbier than others. The old gentleman's directions were spot on I think as I reach the church and find myself on Batley Street. I scan the row of houses, thinking this isn't where I pictured the grand Mrs Mallerby living at all. When I stop at number twenty-five the green front door is peeling and in dire need of a wash.

I can imagine Martha saying, "Being poor is no excuse for being mucky," or something along those lines.

I'm startled now when a neighbour calls, "Nobody's there. Not for these last three months I'd say," before I've even had chance to knock.

She's hanging out of her bedroom window pegging washing on a line which is strewn across the entire width of the street to the opposite house. Three small curious faces stare at me from the ground floor window, with one eating what looks like a slice of dry bread with filthy fingers. All the children look more than a little unkempt. Once more I think this is not the area Mrs Mallerby would choose to live. Perhaps it was a case of needs must if her mother cut her off without an allowance when they quarrelled.

How strange we may have more in common than I think after all. She will not have been fortunate enough to have a Martha to take care of her.

"Thank you I'm looking for the home of Mrs Mallerby," I say, unsure if I dare ask more.

She gives me her full attention now, folding her arms to crush a huge bosom which is proving difficult to ignore. I must seize the opportunity to glean more information.

"Do you happen to know where she may have moved to? I'm keen to find her as I have some news which concerns her."

The woman shakes her head, another strand of brown hair falling loose.

"I've no idea, miss but you could try the corner shop. What Millie Stott doesn't know isn't worth knowing, though don't tell her I said so," she says.

She flashes me a broad grin and I can't help but smile back.

"I am grateful for your time, madam, and I bid you good day."

"Right you are, miss, cheerio," she says, in the broadest of accents, closing the window with a slam.

The three sets of children's eyes watch me as I turn to leave. Not one of them breaks a smile and the sight of them is unsettling.

In the corner shop, a person behind the counter whom I assume to be Millie Stott bids me a good morning as I enter. I return the greeting then scour the narrow, cluttered aisles, choosing a newspaper to appear a genuine customer. She looks tiny and swamped by a sea of provisions in front and behind the counter, some pans even hanging above her. The shop smells of a peculiar mix of wood and boiled ham and something else: Soap, I think it is. I don't find it unpleasant.

"The day is very chilly outside, madam," I say, rummaging for my purse to pay.

"Yes, you can tell winter is around the corner," she replies, popping my money in the drawer and offering change, "Just visiting, are you?"

Nodding, I push my purse back into my bag.

The neighbour was right I think, but I'm glad Millie is an inquisitive person.

"I came to visit a cousin at number twenty-five, but the lady next door told me she moved out a while ago. I've been travelling so I was hoping to surprise her," I say.

Millie's beady eyes look me up then down then up again—she clearly doesn't miss a trick. I will feel happy to be on my way before too long.

"If I recall she was only there a few weeks," she says, edging a little closer to me.

"I'm not one to speak out of turn but she left that house in quite a hurry. I heard a rumour that she'd gone up on the moors, but nobody ventures much out that way. I always think there's something off with her when she bobs in. Never has much to say for herself."

Her face drops now, saying, "Begging your pardon, miss, I forgot who you were for a minute."

"That's quite alright," I say, "When was the last time she was in here?"

"I'd say about a week or so ago and perhaps a fortnight before that. I can't remember exactly as I wasn't taking much notice and one day rolls into the other in here," she says.

Nodding, I think even if she's right it could be a week before she next calls into the shop. That's too long to hang around.

"This moor; could you perhaps tell me the way? It is very important that I find her."

"Ay, of course. But you can't possibly walk up there in those," she says, pointing scornfully at my leather boots, "the moorland gets very boggy this time of year."

"Not to worry, I'm sure they'll clean afterwards," I say.

Muddied boots are the least of my concerns I think as I pop my newspaper into my bag.

"Well, I did warn you. Make your way back onto Ovenden Road then head up the hill and where the road forks, go left. Follow that track for about a mile. You'll have to ask again from there. I hope you find her, miss. I should think she'd be chuffed to see you after so long."

"Yes, I hope so and thank you for your help," I say, throwing her a smile over my shoulder as I leave.

Looking down across the town I can see endless lines of chimneys belching smoke into the icy air as I head up the hill. Thankfully, the handful of children have disappeared into the alleyways and there are only a few people out and about as I head out of town.

I certainly wasn't expecting to trudge up hill and down dale to find Mrs Mallerby, I think as I reach the fork on the road. My steady uphill climb has left my feet raw from the chafing leather boots but I'm determined not to let anything get in the way of tracking down my quarry.

Now, the silent moorland stretches out ahead, and I just can't help my mind wandering to Dicken and our time meeting at the shepherd's hut. I swallow and walk on trying to fend off the memories of a time I'd rather forget.

The track becomes increasingly indistinct the further I go, sporadic clumps of heather blocking a straight route forward. The thinning path has become slippery underfoot and the clouds have descended to almost touch the ground. I have never felt so far from civilisation or comfort.

At the first farmstead I reach, the animals announce my arrival long before I knock on the door. A middle-aged man appears in overalls and wellingtons, taking off his cap when he sees me. The smell of cooked bacon welcomes me.

"Good morning, sir, please forgive my intrusion but may I enquire if you have seen a fair-haired lady passing the farm of late. She's my cousin and I mean to pay her a visit. I have it on good authority she's moved to the area recently but unfortunately, I have mislaid the address."

He laughs gently and I smile but don't understand why he finds this funny.

"By good authority, I take it you mean Millie from the shop," he puts his hand up to stop me explaining, "Ay, as it happens, I've seen a blonde-haired lass passing but I've no idea where you might find her."

My initial disappointment fades quickly. I'm pleased to discover Millie hasn't sent me on a wild goose chase at least.

"If I were you, I'd try Raven's Cottage about a mile up yonder. I've got some boots if you'd care to borrow them, miss," he says, nodding in the direction of my now sodden and muddied footwear. They're my wife's, but she'll not mind, and you can drop them in on your way back to town."

I hesitate a moment as he watches me. I don't wish to cause offence and my feet are frozen and wet through, so I see sense.

"That would be most kind, thank you. I'm sure I shan't be long, but the ground is boggier than I realised," I tell him.

Chuckling to himself, he waves me off as I try to walk in his wife's ill-fitting boots. My feet swim around inside them but at least they're dry.

After about twenty minutes I see a building to my left and a crude sign next to a gate stating *Raven's Cottage*. It's a small holding by the look of it with scarcely enough land to farm. I knock a number of times but I'm unable to rouse anyone, even after checking outside.

Once behind the cottage, dropping down a ridge I spot another farm. I trudge down then a veiny-faced woman, drying her hands on her apron, opens the door to me. Her mouth drops at my unusual attire; an expression I'm becoming accustomed to during my time in Halifax.

"Yes, I've definitely seen a lass who fits your description. I think she's up Glebe Farm," she says after I offer my explanation for landing on her doorstep, "A man called Robinson took on the land, but the house stood empty until a few months back. I've been a bit worried about her now the weather's turning bad if truth be told, but it's not for me to interfere."

She looks at me a moment and then wistfully towards the heavy sky.

"Are you visiting? If you are I can get my Eric to take you there on his horse and cart if you like. It's a good two miles up to Glebe."

How wonderfully amenable the people are out here, I think, a breath of fresh air.

"I'm grateful to you, madam, but I couldn't impose," I say out of politeness.

I'm not keen on another two miles of walking in these ill-fitting wellingtons but I would feel a nuisance taking her up on her offer.

"Now, if I were you, I'd snatch my hand off as you have a fair trek ahead. It will be no bother for him. I'm Mavis, Mavis Thompson, by the way and my husband's name is Eric."

She extends her hand and I shake it, saying now, "Serena, Wilton-Robbins, very pleased to make your acquaintance."

She kicks off her house shoes and changes into her outdoor boots before joining me outside.

"This way, if you will, please, miss."

Eric Thompson is eating a large wedge of cake, his legs dangling from his cart as we approach. He's just about to share a corner of his lunch with his horse, when he stops and looks our way with the same expression his wife had moments ago.

"Eric this is Miss Wilton…," she pauses to look at me.

"Robbins," I say, "But please call me Serena."

"Well, Serena is trying to find her cousin. She thinks she might be that bonny lass up at Glebe. Will you take her up?"

"Will do," Eric says, wiping his hands on his overalls before scrabbling down from his cart to assist me up, "Up you go, miss."

I thank him then turn to watch his wife tramping down the mud path to return to the warmth of her kitchen. She waves without turning around. Oh, to have her simple life right at this moment.

"Well now, it's not every day you come across a well-turned-out young lady with wellingtons and a travel bag out this way. I hope this cousin of yours appreciates the lengths you've gone to is all I can say."

His eyes twinkle as he says it and I smile broadly.

"I'll just be glad to find her," I tell him, "I'm most grateful for your trouble this morning, sir."

"Call me Eric," he says cheerily.

I've warmed to him immediately, no airs and graces like Martha. I can't deny how pleased I am now not to be walking this boggy dirt track. I peer over the side, smelling the wet earth being turned over by the horse's hooves and the cartwheels.

Bouncing around together in the cart for about half an hour, Eric finally raises his crooked finger to point out Glebe Farm to our left. The farmhouse appears above a tall but spindly and crooked hedgerow, battered by the moorland wind and grown bare for winter. The roof is patched, and the doors and windows have all but lost their coat of paint. Hope fades immediately that Mrs Mallerby could be living here in such conditions.

Eric turns to look at me, his eyes watering and his nose reddened from the cold.

"I know what you're thinking, and I agree, the place is a bit of a shambles. I haven't been up here in years."

I take in my surroundings, the bleak vastness of the terrain.

"I'll hang about to see if your cousin comes to the door. If she does, I'll leave, if not, we can both head back down," he says.

He helps me from the cart, and I clomp up the broken bricks of the pathway to the front door. I can't imagine a human being could live here the state the place is in.

I knock. Nothing happens, nobody appears so I try again, fast losing hope. Turning around I see Eric watching me from his cart. He waves my way somehow extending his encouragement and I try one last time.

Hollow footsteps steadily grow louder then come to a standstill. I press my ear to the door. These are not the footsteps of a woman, I think. The door now opens so quickly it startles me and I jump back.

A man in his late twenties pulls his head back when he sees me waiting. He doesn't speak, his expression inhospitable, hostile even as I try now to recover from the shock.

"Yes," he asks.

He's clearly not a gentleman by his brusque manner. The broadness of him almost fills the open doorway. I feel intimidated by him already.

"Good morning, sir, I apologise for disturbing you but may I ask if a Mrs Mallerby lives here by any chance? I am her cousin from Hebden Bridge come visiting," I say attempting to keep my voice light.

One eyebrow raises ever so slightly, and I think he's taken aback by my refined accent. His colourless hair is too long, his clothes stained but of decent quality, all contradicting his standing.

"No, I live here alone. You've had a wasted journey."

His accent is thick. Perhaps he works the land I wonder but the land looks neglected. He stares at me, so I feel a heat up my back stopping at my cheeks. My forced smile will be too wide and too fixed to convince him.

"Ah, I see, then in that case I will leave you to your morning, sir," I say.

I quickly steal a glance over his shoulder, but his face turns to one side following my eyes. I was careless and now he's caught me in the act. His neck cranes further, so he knows I've spotted a fine woollen coat over the back of a chair, far too small to fit a man. His face swings back in my direction as if on a hinge, so I deliberately turn to look at Eric still waiting on the cart at the end of the path. Oh, Eric I'm so glad you're here, I think.

"I bid you good morning and apologise for the interruption to your day," I say, backing away from the door as I speak.

A pregnant pause causes me to turn and pick up speed to get away from this man. There's something decidedly unpleasant about his manner.

I try not to run now back to the safe harbour that is Eric and his horse and cart. As he helps me up, I keep my eyes forward, away from the direction of the house. When Eric clicks his tongue against his cheek and flaps the reins to set us in motion, I'm so relieved.

I've yet to hear the farmhouse door closing.

"No luck then I take it. I thought it was a bit of a long shot judging by the state of it here. This is no place for a lady to live."

I can't speak. I see Eric steal a look at me from the corner of my eye, but I don't respond.

"Is everything alright, miss, you look fair winded?" he asks.

My stomach is tight, my top lip wet, so I dab it with my handkerchief and let out a breath of air.

"I'm sorry, Eric, I can't quite put my finger on why, but I feel so affected by the encounter with that man. I don't believe for a minute he lives alone. I saw a woman's coat on the chair back and his manner was … unsettling."

"Unsettling; in what way?"

I purse my lips trying to think how to describe what I mean.

"I think you would understand more if you'd been there, he had an air of menace. He's certainly no farmer."

It was more of a feeling, an instinct, so I'm finding it difficult to explain.

"You're making a lot of presumptions after one short conversation if you don't mind me saying so. I hardly think a coat and a brief if odd conversation would be classed as hard and fast evidence," he says.

Eric laughs but he doesn't convince me. Nor does he put my mind at rest.

Raising a smile as best I can to move away from the subject, I undoubtedly agree my argument sounds weak. Regardless, I shan't be heading back to Hebden Bridge today. I must instead send Martha a telegraph to inform her of my delay.

No matter how farfetched it sounds to my new friend I would be foolish to ignore such a powerful instinct.

Something is dreadfully wrong at Glebe Farm; I just know it.

Chapter 19

I hate to be away from my loved ones at Mallerby Hall any longer than necessary, but my current situation is just that: a necessity.

If I draw a blank after further investigations into the occupants of Glebe Farm, I can live with that easier than not investigating at all. As Martha says, you rarely regret what you do, it's what you don't do that will keep you up at night.

Eric invites me in when we arrive back at Moss Farm. I'm keen to get on but he and Mavis have been so helpful it would seem rude to refuse his offer.

As we share a warming cup of tea and an overly generous slab of fruit loaf, I ask if they know of any rooms in Halifax they might recommend.

"Well, let's see, there's the *Hare & Hounds*, they have plenty of rooms," Mavis tells me.

She butters the fruit loaf with expert hands and puts the tray in the middle of the table.

"You're set on finding out more, I take it," Eric chips in.

The farmhouse is basic, but pristine and Mavis obviously likes to keep a nice house. The range is blazing cheerily away, and I'm at home already.

I nod, biting into my fruit loaf as Eric watches me. He sighs, sitting back in his chair.

"You might be right, there's nowhere else the blonde lass could be living up there, I know all the other farmers. Now, you're sure you've got the right place?" he asks.

"It's all I have to go on," I respond, realising I'm pinning everything on the word of a gossip: Millie at the corner shop.

"You were saying she still visits the shop down the valley, so I suppose we could wait and see. She'll have to pass here in any case, there's no other way. I can call at the inn to tell you where she goes. She doesn't pass every day, mind so you might have to wait."

I'm touched he would go to such lengths for a stranger.

"I can't tell you how much I would appreciate any help you could give me, Eric."

He glugs down the contents of his mug then bangs the empty cup on the table.

"Right, well you won't be able to sit in your room all day. I know a lady called Dorothy who runs *The Silver Spoon*. I'll tell her you've come for some country air to have a rest. She'll see you right. Come on, lass let's drop your wellies back before old Johnny's wife misses them and comes storming up the track after you."

We all share a chuckle and I promise Mavis I'll return.

"I hope you do, Miss Serena," she says, helping me on with my coat.

I look at them both as I head out the door. There's just something about the worn, weathered faces of the two strangers which made it the easiest thing in the world to entrust them with my secret.

*

My room at the *Hare & Hounds* is lacking in home comforts but more importantly it is affordable, at least for a few days and I'm relieved to find that a supper of bread, broth and chicken is included. During the day I venture to the tearoom Eric mentioned, wiling away the hours in my book. I'm distracted every time the tearoom doorbell chimes so I look up, only to be deflated when I see it's not Eric.

This has been the same for the last two days and I don't know how much longer I can wait or how my purse will last. I'm on full alert but still missing home, my emotions heightened.

I have people I miss dearly waiting for me to come home.

"Refill?" Dorothy asks, teapot in hand.

"Thank you," I say though I'm awash with tea. The air is far too damp to sit outdoors so I tramp between the tearoom and the inn when my restlessness becomes too much.

"It's a pity you didn't come in the summer, miss," Dorothy says, filling my cup, "But then I don't suppose you can pick and choose when you need a rest."

She smiles wryly making me wonder if she's twigged there's far more to my story than I've disclosed.

I've discovered so much about Dorothy over the last two days: She went to school with Eric and Mavis before she married Thomas. He died some ten years ago she tells me, so the little tearoom is a lifeline in many ways, not least because she's a person who likes the company of people. She's not bothered about another man because her husband in her words was a "right pain in the rearend." She dresses comfortably with two coiled plaits at the side of her ears which resemble earmuffs, wearing men's shoes under her dress because she's on her feet all day.

"I'd not have another man if he was dipped in sugar," she told me on the first day, making me almost choke on my tea.

The door chimes again as she walks away, and I almost look back down at my book until this time I'm finally met by a sight for sore eyes: Eric, flat cap in hand, dodging the tables and chairs to reach me.

"Dorothy," he says, nodding in her direction, "Miss Serena, the missus has asked if you'd care to join us for tea. I'm sure you'd be glad of the change of scenery, no offence, Dorothy."

"None taken, Eric. I say, get yourself off and have a nice time, miss. I wouldn't mind a bit of Mavis's cooking myself."

Eric looks at me then rolls his eyes towards the door and back again, clearly some code to get my attention. I must make haste as he obviously has news. Opening my purse, Dorothy shakes her head telling me she can run to a few cups of tea and a bun for a friend of a friend. I'm sure she has guessed more about my situation.

"I'm grateful to you, Dorothy," I say over my shoulder, trying not to rush to keep up with Eric who's now striding towards the door.

"You're welcome at ours any time, Dorothy," Eric says, and she raises her hand in farewell.

The street is quiet, due to the cold snap and most are indoors as it's teatime.

Eric puts his cap on, and I trot by his side until he realises then slows his pace.

"I thought she might have scarpered after you called at the house, but a blonde lass finally went past as I was feeding the sheep in the lower field. I've been keeping a good look out, but she's changed her route down here. I had to fair run down the moor to catch her up. She didn't see me, I was careful about it."

He nods in the direction of Millie's shop.

"Oh, Eric, how can I ever thank you," I say, touching his arm.

If I thought it wouldn't embarrass him, I'd kiss his cheek. I'm so delighted after two endless days of waiting.

He pats my hand on his arm briefly then shuffles from foot to foot.

"Now, there's no need for that I'm glad to help. I'll hang about for a bit then slope off if all goes to plan, but in any case, I'd be grateful for a report back when you get chance."

"Of course," I say as I back away to take my position, "I'll see you both soon, Eric, I promise. I'll never forget how you and Mavis have gone out of your way to help me."

He touches my elbow as I turn, so I stop mid-step. His face is so set I wonder what he's about to disclose.

"Now mind how you go, miss. I mean it now, don't be silly about it, you're only a bairn when all said and done."

"I won't be a hero if this is what you're thinking, don't worry, Eric."

He heads back down the street to a bench seat. He will look decidedly out of place in the drizzle which has just started.

Ensconced in Dorothy's café for days I've had plenty of time to plan the best spot to wait for Mrs Mallerby coming out of the shop. In my mind I've pictured every scenario which might unfold when she sees me but I'm still unprepared now the moment is almost upon us.

I can hear the shop bell chime from where I'm standing. It rings more than once, and I step back around the corner to watch. Twice the customer must have gone the other way home, so I don't see them and once an older woman appears.

Minutes pass until I hear it again. I wait, holding my breath.

I see her. She's walking quickly, basket in hand, wearing a dark woollen coat and hat. In the fading light it's as though she's trying to be invisible. I see the merest sighting of blonde hair falling from under her hat. Is this the woman I've been searching for? How I hope so.

I must make my move, it's now or never, I think stepping into the street and quickening my pace to move alongside her.

"Mrs Mallerby," I say.

There's no response. Either it's not her or it is and she hasn't heard.

"Mrs Mallerby," I say louder this time.

She comes to a sudden halt, turning around but not slowly.

The look of sheer horror on her face under the streetlamp as she turns tells me everything I need to know.

Chapter 20

As I watch her across the carriage, I can't quite believe she's real, that she's really here. I'm almost expecting her to disappear in a puff of smoke any moment.

There in the seat opposite and only inches away from me is the wife of the man I love. This woman is no longer an enigmatic stranger, a woman who lived in my mind almost to the point of obsession. She has now become a living, breathing person.

She raises a tight smile, her eyes glazed before she resumes her study of the landscape beyond the window. Her face is pale and strained in profile, the veins of her long neck protruding slightly.

For so long I have wanted to know every detail about this woman, but this is not how I pictured her or our union. Perhaps one should be mindful of one's curiosity.

Dawson will not be happy with me to say the least. He will see my interference as overstepping the mark, involving myself in matters which do not concern me, and I can't argue. But time will roll by, and he'll come to understand my intentions were honourable, my actions only for the greater good. I have nothing to gain by reinstating his wife in the matrimonial home.

He shan't throw me out I know that at least. He will sulk perhaps or retreat for a while to lick his wounds. I am the one who must endure the cold reality of unrequited love. I have chosen to be the loser, and Alicia Mallerby sitting opposite is indeed the winner.

Was it only yesterday when I waylaid her on the street. She must have thought she'd become anonymous, so how could a stranger possibly know her name? Anonymity however clearly hasn't brought her happiness.

"Please, I come only as a friend, I don't wish to alarm you," I quickly reassured her, "My name is Serena. I work for your husband, and I'm keen to speak with you if you'll allow it. I've been searching for you."

She saw I was a lady; but must therefore have wondered in what capacity could I possibly work for her husband? Yet to say simply that I knew her husband would have connotations. Connotations which sadly would have been founded. I've decided she must never find out about my lapse in judgement.

"Has something happened to my husband?" she asked.

Her voice was breathy as though she was winded. That she would think this hadn't occurred to me … yet I had further reassurance I was doing the right thing. Her expression was one of concern.

"No, your husband is well. I promise I will explain everything to you, Mrs Mallerby if you'll only spare me a moment of your time."

This woman needed my help; I was sure of it even then.

"How on earth did you find me, it certainly can't have been easy?" she asked.

"Well, I paid your mother a visit as my first port of call."

"My mother! My, you have been busy," she gave me a steady look, "I wonder why you should care so much."

I had no idea how to answer; I felt ensnared. The rain was seeping steadily into my coat, the provisions in her basket swathed with raindrops, both spurring me to ask the question.

"I have a room at the *Hare & Hounds*. Would you come shelter there with me just for a short while?"

Panic swept across her face.

"No, I must return home and soon," she said.

I was brave, I hadn't got so far down the path to give up easily.

"Will you be in trouble if you don't return home soon?" I asked.

Her eyes tumbled to the floor, her flushed cheeks giving her away.

"I shan't be in trouble, but I don't see what we must discuss. My husband and I have been apart for many years," she said.

She was backing away from me, and also from the conversation. I was losing her.

"Please, don't leave just yet," I said.

My voice was sharper than I intended but I couldn't let her go.

I watched her biting her bottom lip. Was she tempted I wondered. Should I cajole her some more? I decided to stay quiet, my breath curling in a tight ball between my breasts waiting for her response.

She sighed then, taking one step towards me.

"I can give you ten minutes before I must return home."

"Of course, I understand," I told her.

I prayed this would allow me enough time. Following me in the direction of the inn, she looked constantly around her as though someone might appear at any moment. I knew only too well who the person was, and I felt sorry for her because I understood why she would feel that way entirely from my own encounter.

Eric raised his thumb discreetly before returning to Mavis and his farm on the moors. This morning I woke thinking what an ally and protector he has been. I shall never forget it.

The inn was quiet before the arrival of the evening regulars. We climbed the back stairs to the comfort and shelter of my small room where I lit the fire laid in preparation for my return and removed my wet hat and coat.

"Would you like me to dry your things?" I asked.

She shook her head before glancing around the room and perching on a chair by the fire which was flickering to life. I sat on the edge of the bed as there was only one chair.

I cleared my throat. My next words were crucial in pushing ahead with my plan.

"I don't wish to keep you sitting in your wet things, so I will get straight to the point. I of course have my own story, but this is not important at present. I've been working for your husband at Mallerby Hall for some months and during this time I've become convinced he would like to speak with you about your circumstances."

She gave a low laugh.

"I'm sorry to break it to you but I think you may have been on a fool's errand, Miss …"

"Wilton-Robbins; Serena," I said.

"I'm sorry Miss Wilton-Robbins but I very much doubt this to be the case."

I blushed knowing this was the truth of the matter, but knowing she would leave if I said as much.

"I'm certain he still loves you," I said, my urgent tone adding to the sincerity of my words.

She sat quietly for a moment until she suddenly pushed a hand to her mouth.

"He still loves me; but how could you possibly know?"

I'm convincing her, I can feel it.

"I know because I see it in his eyes. I know because of the way he looks when he reads your letters. I somehow know he will be taken by surprise but eventually he will be glad for me to bring you back home with me tomorrow, today if you wish."

I was taking a gamble, but I'd come to understand Dawson Mallerby in the months we'd been companions and more. He has unfinished marital business with his beautiful wife and the signs told me his feelings were reciprocated.

"Would you like to return to Mallerby Hall?" I asked her.

She looked down at her hands grasped tightly together in her lap for the longest time while I tried not to think about my future at the hall should she return.

Finally, she sighed then removed her gloves to undo the top button of her coat. She removed her hat to place it on the hearth, showing me a hue of golden hair.

I had my answer.

"I'm suddenly very hungry, I think we should eat," she said, taking the provisions one by one from her basket.

I smiled with relief, then pulled a small table between us as she laid out some bread and cheese and even some beer that she must have bought for the man she lives with. We tore hunks of bread and pulled cheese to nibble then washed it down with the beer as we talked by the fire.

She listened intently as I related my fall from grace. She didn't comment or even judge—she couldn't—she only let me tell my story. My heart was broken, and she could understand because her heart was broken too.

Then with her trust cemented I think, she told me her own tale of heartbreak as I devoured every word.

"Larry was the supervisor at the factory. He was Dawson's loyal and trusted right-hand man and they'd worked together for ten years, even before our marriage. Our paths crossed regularly at the factory and the hall. There was something about his brooding demeanour that drew me. He was different then. I often wonder if that person was the real Larry or if I'm living with him now. Either way, he became an obsession at a time when I felt Dawson and I were drifting apart. I couldn't ignore it and without going into detail, one day fate intervened when we found ourselves alone at the empty factory.

But the guilt after my interlude with Larry was terrible, driving me to end my relationship with him. I went to stay at my mother's in the hope of ridding him from my mind. It wasn't working and then one day he landed on the doorstep, and I knew when I saw him how deeply I felt. It transpired he felt the same and though I knew it was wrong I was relieved."

She took a sip of beer from her teacup.

"Dawson was never my mother's favourite person, he's so different from my father who spent more time at home with us. However, she could never condone an adulterous relationship.

"Alicia," she said, "I have allowed you to hide away in this house for too long. You must face the consequences and clean up your own mess." It was the right thing even though I didn't want to hear at the time."

As Alicia wiped a tear with her finger, I hurried to find a clean handkerchief from my bag. Smiling at me weakly she took it, burying her face in the white cotton and lace a moment. I stayed silent while she composed herself.

"Larry left the mill and we moved to the house on Batley Street, living on a little money he had put by. I clearly couldn't expect Dawson to maintain me, and mother had cut off the small allowance she provided after I went to stay with her.

At first it was something of an adventure. I did love him, but I also loved Dawson in the same way: passionately. Yes, Dawson had always been a distant husband, dedicated to the running of the factory but I knew he loved me. His work is demanding, and he's determined to keep the legacy of his father's hard work alive and ensure the factory flourishes for the workers as much for himself. My days at Mallerby Hall were long and dull and Larry was a welcome distraction. Now I know the only real love Larry has, is for something I can never compete with. He's an inveterate gambler—cards, horses, dogs, you name something, and he will wager it."

She sighed, closing her eyes.

"I'm not proud of myself, you understand, but then I'm not the first to fall in love the wrong person and I won't be the last."

She's right of course. It's very easy to be fooled if you want to be.

"It upset me more because Larry told me he started gambling to try and impress me and keep me in the style I was accustomed. Dawson let him go of course and he found it difficult to secure a similar job without references. I think I would have been happy with say, a millworker's salary but Larry laughed when I told him. Perhaps he was right to. Oh, Serena, perhaps I did drive him to gambling."

Her expression made me reach across for her hand.

"A person must take responsibility for their own actions, Alicia," I said, "This side of him would have come out sooner or later, it will have always been there waiting to show itself."

"Perhaps you're right but in any case, our money frittered away daily like sand in an hourglass."

I remembered Martha quoting another of her mother's famous homilies: When money flies out the door, love flies out the window. How wise she was.

"Eventually we were unable to pay the rent in Batley Street, so we moved to the near derelict farm cottage where you found us. Now we're unable to pay the landlord even the measly rent he's asking for that. I'm sure Larry is heading for debtors' prison before too long, but I can't make him see sense. Next time will be the one he tells me, getting angry when I protest."

She looked at me.

"Am I that person? The person who is ruled by money and not by love. I've dreamed about going back home to Dawson, but I'm not sure even now if I would be returning for the security rather than the man," she said turning her head to stare into the flames.

Sitting quietly together a moment the thought hung in the air, but I knew she was the only one who had the answer to that question.

"Are you in love with Dawson?" I asked.

I wanted to try and simplify her decision so we could find the way forward.

Her smile was tired, the firelight aglow in her blue eyes.

"I am in love with him," she said, shaking her head slightly as though realising it for the first time in a long while.

"So, will you stay here tonight and accompany me on the first train home tomorrow?" I asked.

My voice was so quiet it was almost a whisper.

I thought of Eric and Mavis and my promise, but then I thought of the expression on Larry's face as he opened the door to me two days before. I decided to write a letter care of Dorothy and pop it under the door of *The Silver Spoon*. One day I will return I vowed.

"Will Larry come look for you?" I asked.

She shrugged.

"He might but he won't be home until late and even then, he won't think of trying here because he knows I have no money. This would be a safe place to stay tonight."

I somehow had to ask.

"Did … did he ever raise his hand to you?"

Standing she shook the crumbs from her skirts onto the hearth then sat down again to pile the cups and saucers we used for our food, avoiding looking my way.

"He came close a time or two and now after our talk I realise it was only going to be a matter of time before he did. His pride is hanging by a thread."

The threat of violence is almost as bad, I thought. Moira struck me more than once, but the sense of dread and foreboding in the atmosphere of the house made life just as miserable.

When I took her hand in mine, she didn't pull away.

"I'm offering you a way out, Alicia," I said, "and if I were you, I'd take it and come home if only for a while. Surely you owe it yourself to close this chapter of your life with Dawson properly if nothing else and you could then make a fresh start."

She smiled and I thought how this lady had offloaded so much of herself to a stranger. The only thing she hadn't mentioned were the losses she and Dawson have lived through. Some things are just too distressing or private to speak of, better left unsaid.

Turning to me she said: "And you. You have obviously been dreadfully let down by this Dicken fellow but it has given you a gift of wisdom when it comes to matters of the heart, Serena."

"Is that a "yes", are we going home together?" I asked, the corners of my mouth twitching.

"Home; what an evocative word," she said.

Oh, the bitter-sweet relief. Come what may, the next part of our lives can begin.

Lifting her eyes from our entwined hands she looked directly into mine so intensely I was unsettled for a moment.

"I only pray your wisdom and instincts turn out to be right, Serena… for both our sakes."

Chapter 21

When Mr Slater opens the door to see me standing there with Alicia, there isn't even a glimmer of surprise. It's as if he has been waiting for us.

"Good morning, madam; Mrs Robson," he says standing to one side to allow us entry to the hall.

Martha rushes towards us, arms extended.

"Let me get you out of that coat, madam, you must be freezing," she says.

They're treating their mistress as though she's just returned from a brisk morning walk around the park.

I glance at Alicia who looks like a little girl lost in her own hallway. She has no luggage, her dress is worn and grubby, all so far removed from the day she left I imagine.

I watched her brush her hair this morning with fascination. Is it any wonder she was spotted around Halifax with such a crowning glory?

Martha takes her mistress's coat then beams my way. She looks proud of me, as though I've come home with a prize for excellent handwriting from the teacher. I have so much I want to tell her, discuss with her, but it will have to keep for now.

"Shall I run you a hot bath, madam, it's parky out there today and it will be just the thing to warm you up nicely?" she asks slipping into what I'm sure was their old routine with ease.

"That would be lovely, thank you, Martha," Alicia says.

She mounts the stairs ahead of Martha, then stops midway to turn around. Mr Slater has left to continue his tasks, so it's just the three of us.

"Thank you too, Serena," she says, quietly "I am glad to be home."

Martha smiles fondly my way.

"Rest now. You have all afternoon to prepare yourself," I say, already taking my first steps towards the scullery staircase.

Racing down the stairs I rush to the crib by the kitchen range. Safe and snug, my little daughter has been in the best hands with Martha in my prolonged absence. For once, I don't worry about waking her as I take her into my arms and breathe her sweet baby scent.

"How I've missed you, my darling. I promise Mama will never leave you again, you have my word," I whisper as she opens her eyes and gives me a sleepy smile. I rock her gently for a while.

"Mrs Robson, how nice it is to see you back from your travels safe and sound," Mr Slater says.

I was so preoccupied with my reunion with Hannah, I didn't hear him come down the stairs.

He pulls his suit sleeves down his arm to align with his cuffs, his awkwardness now we're alone immediately apparent.

"How kind of you to say so, Mr Slater," I tell him swaying gently still, "Thank you for taking such good care of my daughter whilst I've been away."

Martha comes down the stairs as Mr Slater steps out of her way. If only my affections could be transferred to this man, I think, I know all our troubles would be over.

Yet unlike Alicia I know without a shadow of a doubt I'm not that woman she spoke of; a woman whose driving force is not love.

"Excuse me if you will, I must check the wine for this evening," Mr Slater says, heading off to the cellar.

Martha's eyes twinkle as he leaves making it clear what she's thinking, then she nods towards the table and freshly made Victoria sponge cake waiting in the centre for our homecoming. The smell of this room is home.

"Well, that's the mistress down for a long nap. I know you'll have plenty to tell me but I'm in the same boat," Martha says.

Sitting with Hannah on my knee I offer my daughter some cake and she pushes it into her mouth with a grin.

"Well, lass, I'm afraid you must brace yourself for a shock," Martha says reaching to smooth Hannah's hair, "that Dicken fellow has been round again. He came the day before yesterday, and I can't imagine he came with your best interests at heart. I've had to play dumb with the master as to where you've been, but I suppose it will all become clear to him before the days out. I can't believe you managed to persuade her to come home, I had my doubts and plenty of them."

Martha's quick-fire delivery of all that has happened means I'm struggling to keep up. But when I do, I realise she has been put in a very awkward position with her employer.

"Oh, Martha how dreadful for you, I've been hoping you wouldn't land in hot water in my absence. As for Dicken, it doesn't take a genius to work out why he came calling. He will have been thrown when he discovered I wasn't here."

Stirring the sugar in her tea she nods her head.

"You're not wrong. Mr Dicken asked to speak to you first when he came. He was stone cold sober this time, arriving all gentlemanly like and he went into the study with the master. I thought they might ask me to take Hannah in to see them, but I don't think Mr Mallerby would do that without your permission," she raises her eyes to heaven, "Lord only knows what they think you've been doing while you've been away, but I tell you something for nothing, they would never be able to guess."

"Thank you for covering for me, Martha, at least I succeeded in bringing Mrs Mallerby home. I've decided to speak to Mr Mallerby when I go clean at Millthwaite's later though I doubt I'll get to the cleaning. I thought it best to pave the way about his wife's return, so he's forewarned. I can't say I'm looking forward to it, but it's only what I expected to happen."

"I'd like to be a fly on the wall for that conversation, I would that. He'll have a right shock. The mistress looks a shadow of her former self though, fair miserable. I bet she wondered why you went to all the trouble."

"She did, Martha," I say wiping the crumbs from Hannah's mouth, "But then I think I got there just in time."

I tell Martha about Alicia's quarrel with her mother but make no mention of the other man in Alicia's life: Martha has been placed in far too many compromising situations already. This certainly isn't something she needs to know about, and I already feel a loyalty to Alicia.

I would be betraying her confidence in disclosing too much.

*

At teatime I put on my coat to take the long walk to Millthwaite's feeling like I'm heading to the gallows. Oh, the trouble I've started, but it's too late to be thinking about that now.

Miss Rutland is walking up the yard to the front gates as I approach from the woods at the rear. I'm thankful to be spared the cold interaction for once and especially this evening.

The hush of the factory after the hustle and bustle of the day is usually my favourite time. The lamp at Dawson's desk is glowing cosily through the mullioned window as I unbutton my coat and remove my hat and gloves. I watch him a moment with his head bowed, diligently working and completely unaware of the change I've brought about in his life.

I no longer knock nowadays when we're alone, so I startle him when I step into the room. His face lights up as I close the door behind me, and I look away from it like a scorching sunshine. I'm unable to muster a smile as I can't help but pre-empt the conversation.

"Serena, you're back. One more day and I'd have sent a search party out for you," he says with a small laugh.

He's only half-joking, I know he will have been worried.

If only I could be near him, I would settle immediately. But this is no longer possible, that boat has sailed. Instead, I sit in the leather chair by the hearth and fuss with my skirts, my favourite trick to bide time.

"Forgive my unannounced and mysterious disappearance. I've had a trying few days away, but thankfully I succeeded in what I set out to do."

He tilts his head, but his mouth has set in a line. He looks as though he's starting to brace himself for news.

"I see. So now can you tell me where you have been these past few days?"

Closing my eyes, I search for my first word.

"I will explain but before I do I think you must prepare yourself for a shock or … or perhaps a surprise might be a better word."

His face tightens more as he wanders to the front of his desk, separating his coattails and perching on the edge.

"You have my full attention," he says, his eyes trying to hold mine.

Our world has changed; I have changed it. His world is better though he doesn't know it yet, whereas mine will not be. I will be cast adrift and must think of alternative arrangements soon if I'm to survive this predicament.

I look down at the rug and take a breath through my nose, feeling quite sick.

"I left with a mission. However, you must understand that although it will take the wind from your sails my intention was only to help restore your happiness."

His eyes narrow and the bone at the side of his ear moves up and down quickly but he remains silent. I must spit out my confession and be done with it.

"I went in search of your wife with… with the purpose of bringing her home to talk to you if she would."

There, I've said it. He looks at me blankly for a second or two. I watch him digest the impact of my admission, running his hand down his face, then rubbing the back of his neck.

I don't want him to speak.

"You had no right to do such a thing on my behalf, Serena. I'm disappointed, you should have spoken to me first before you set off on your little ... escapade. Now a line has been crossed; *you* have crossed a line."

His tone is quiet, measured, his voice thin and expressionless. Somehow this is worse than him shouting. He stands to walk back to his chair, the desk now acting as a barrier between us. Mr Mallerby is now my employer, not a lover or a friend even.

He picks up his pen and pretends to refocus his attention on the document he was writing. Everything is different since the last time he looked at it.

"I would be grateful if you could return to the house. I've nothing more to say to you this evening," he says tersely, then adding as an afterthought, "I must be allowed time to think."

I stare at the top of his head, his hair in perfect waves. I notice his pen has yet to move across the page.

My legs are at risk of buckling, but I manage to make my way across the room. All the while his eyes never leave the paper. You are treading on quicksand, Serena Wilton-Robins, I think. The shame I feel threatens to overwhelm me as I close the door and head home dejected, rejected.

Of all the reactions I had anticipated from Dawson Mallerby—fury, bemusement, elation even—disappointment was never a consideration.

And yet it's the one that stings the most.

Chapter 22

The room has been silent too long.

Any moment I may need to dash to the under-stair cupboard to hide. But until such time I remain pinned with my back to the wall.

I have yet to see Dawson since he returned home. I've been wise enough to keep out of his way and Martha stoked the fires in his room until she retired to bed.

"Well, you did all you did with goodness in your heart, Little Robin," she said holding me in her embrace when I returned home in tears, "The master will see this in time, don't fret now."

"I wish I'd listened to you when you tried to talk me out of it, Martha."

She held me at arm's length and bobbed down to look at my lowered face.

"It might not work out for them but then it might; either way they'll know for sure. You told me this yourself and I understand. But I think the mistress will thank you. She's his wife and she was sinking and now he will see it for himself. Come on, dry your eyes and we'll have a cup of tea. We know everything is always better after a cup of tea."

I dried my eyes and tried to smile though my heart hung like a weight.

I went upstairs to see Alicia in her room after I managed to pull myself together.

"Here you are at last, Serena, I've been pacing the floor," she said the moment I crossed the threshold.

I had few words of comfort to offer. I could have lied but somehow, I already find it impossible and what would be the point?

When we arrived, she looked like she didn't belong but this evening she was restored to being the lady of the house, in her dark blue brocade evening gown, complimenting her pretty hair coiled at the crown. She was wearing pearls and matching earrings, her eyes bright and refreshed from her afternoon nap. So many times, I'd imagined the dresses hung in the wardrobes and the woman who wore them.

Conversation was difficult as we awaited Dawson's arrival. I went backwards and forwards to the window too many times.

Eventually Alicia looked at me almost coyly.

"Would you bring your daughter to meet me?" she asked.

I wasn't sure if it was the right thing for her to meet my baby daughter. It would surely flood her with painful memories.

"Do you really want to meet her now; would it not be better to wait?" I asked.

Craning in my seat, I glanced once more out of the window to check if Dawson was on his way.

"Of course, now is the perfect time" she said, "I think Hannah may be just the distraction we need. Sitting here is simply torture."

We shared a smile, and I left the room to fetch Hannah.

When I stooped to pick her up from the rug, Martha also asked me if I thought it a good idea.

"No, but Mrs Mallerby was insistent. I suppose she will have to meet her some time," I told her.

"This could go awry, Serena" she said, "It's too much too soon if you ask me."

I raised my eyes and shrugged. What alternative did I have but to resign myself to dealing with any upset sooner or later?

I could only stand and wait with Hannah in my arms in Alicia's room. I had no idea what to do or say. I was out of my depth, and wished I'd had the foresight to bring Martha with me. She always knows the right thing to say.

Alicia walked towards both of us with the brightest of smiles on her face. Her expression was only marred by the tears glistening in her eyes.

"She is indeed a beautiful baby, Serena," she said, "And she looks so like her mother. Everyone must say this when they meet her," she said.

"Yes, it has been said once or twice," I said laughing, glad of the release.

She stroked her forefinger over Hannah's cheek, lost in her thoughts and perhaps her memories.

"I have many plans for change in this house should Dawson wish me to stay. I hope you turn out to be right and he does," she told me, "I have plans for you too though we must tread very carefully, Serena. Whatever happens we have a long road ahead."

Her expression was heart-breaking. She has been damaged by a situation of her own making, which I think is worse. Only time will help, and time cannot be rushed.

"We will get there, I'm know it," I said.

I had no idea what those changes might be, but I was longing to take the next small step along the long road with them and be done with it.

By the time Dawson returned Alicia had settled herself in the drawing room. It was past nine o'clock, so Alicia and I had eaten together in her room with

Hannah playing at our feet. I sat out my penance, my ears pricking at every noise outside. He had left me to think about the consequences of my actions like a small child.

From the top of the stairs, I heard a polite exchange between Dawson and Alicia before the door closed to the drawing room. Then I snuck down the stairs to assume my position at the door. Listening at keyholes, what new impropriety will you think of next Serena, I wondered.
But I had to listen in; I wasn't going to be left in the dark and have to wait until morning.

They began their conversation in a strangely formal way, enquiring after each other's health; they sounded like complete strangers but after being apart for so long this could be forgiven. The conversation had to begin somewhere and civility is a good place to start.

"How did Serena find you in the end?" Dawson asks after a long silence.

"She was quite the sleuth and very resourceful, even encountering the wrath of my mother as a starting point. You have a good friend in her," Alicia says, her voice sounding different.

He doesn't respond; I didn't expect him to.

I picture them sitting in their respective chairs by the fireside as they will have done many a year before their separation. It seems you can live in the same house as a person and still be distant from your heart and mind.

"Dawson, I'm sorry," she says quietly.

"So, you're sorry and that's that then, Alicia, is it?" he says just as quietly.

"No, of course not."

"Are you foolish enough to think that an apology will allow us to just pick up where we left off; do you consider me such a pushover?"

His voice is louder and now he sounds like a stranger. Silence descends on the room once more.

"You must surely understand, you didn't just leave me, you left me for a man who was more than a trusted employee. Larry was my friend, I lost both of you," he says.

The hurt in his tone is so plain to hear.

My heart hurts. Please consider your response carefully, Alicia, I think.

"I wouldn't have returned at all if it wasn't for Serena's efforts. I didn't think for a moment you would even entertain a conversation with me, let alone allow me back in the house."

"All I ever wanted in the world once was a conversation," he says flatly.

I take a great gulp of air and put my hand to my mouth. How much pain this man has endured. Whatever happens it will be worth it to restore his peace if nothing else.

"Tonight, is not the night to pursue the matter," he says, "We're both tired and I'm not in a the right frame of mind. Perhaps tomorrow will be better."

I run upstairs as I hear Alicia say, "Until tomorrow then, Dawson. If you return earlier from the factory, perhaps we could dine together."

I'm too far away by now to hear his response. What should I do? I decide to wait on the landing for Alicia to come upstairs.

Our eyes lock as she spots me outside her door, her expression serious.

I don't need to ask the question.

"I'm still here and this is more than I could have hoped for yesterday, Serena. I have broken his heart. Only time will tell us if we have a future."

A tear runs down her cheek as she opens the door to her bedroom.

Friend, confidante, servant; somehow, I'm equal to this woman in mind though my circumstances have been reduced. We will be friends come what may I know it already.

I think of Rowena and our friendship at Wentworth now though I try not to. She is the one I miss the most.

So, it seems we all have a terrible price to pay for love.

Chapter 23

Dawson has returned late yet again so Alicia and I dined together again and stayed together until we heard his carriage approaching the hall.

"I'm not going down, Serena, he can request my company if he wishes but I think it better not to force things," she says, "this only has the impetus to make a bad situation worse."

She sits at her dressing table and pumps a cloud of her favourite fragrance at her neck and wrists.

Slightly flustered I'm already enroute to the door. The last thing I want is to run into Dawson, so I dash down the two flights of steps to the scullery as quick as I can.

I watch his feet pass the window of the cellar and stand listening to Mr Slater taking his coat. I can't tell what kind of mood he's in by his tone.

A few minutes later, Martha emerges looking serious.

"Mr Mallerby asks if you will join him in the parlour."

She makes me jump, seeming to sneak up on me. She will have been drawing the curtains for the evening.

"Me; why me and not his wife?" I ask.

My tone is more brittle than intended.

"I'd be glad if you wouldn't shoot the messenger," she says filling the kettle.

"Forgive me, Martha, I'm just a little taken aback. In what frame of mind does he look?

I have no option but to face him I'd prefer not to walk into the lion's den.

"He doesn't look angry if that's what you mean. As you said to me about the mistress meeting Hannah, you'll have to face him some time; it must be hanging over you. Oh, and he's asked if you can take the bairn with you."

This is good news at least. He is always gentle and kind around Hannah.

I knock on the door, tidying Hannah's unruly curls with my fingers. Once in the room I sit Hannah on the hearth rug with her toys. This is our usual routine but nothing about this meeting is usual.

"Well, are you sitting down this evening, I wonder?" he asks, eyes fixed firmly on Hannah.

He's unable to stop his face breaking into a small smile as she hugs Mallers, the bear he bought for her first Christmas, talking to him animatedly in her baby tongue.

I think it best to remain silent. I'd rather not poke a bear, the one with a sore head and antagonise him.

"I'm really at a loss for words. You have placed me in an intolerable position, and I simply don't understand what you were you thinking."

I'm unable to let the comment pass.

"I was thinking of you," I tell him, the words rushing out of my mouth in desperate frustration.

He opens his mouth to speak and then closes it again.

"I don't know what to say to you," he says after reflection, "You appear to have developed a knack for throwing me off-course. But why couldn't you just leave well alone?"

"I'm sorry but things were anything but well and I couldn't stand idly by when it's clear you have unfinished business with your wife…"

He holds his hands up, saying quickly, "Yes, and this is entirely our business, and none of yours."

Though his face is full of fury, I remain steadfast. I must defend myself. My intentions were honest.

"But you were so unhappy apart, Dawson."

I'm horrified as his name slips out of my mouth, but he appears not to notice, only shaking his head.

"Just because we are unhappy apart, does not mean my wife and I will be happy together. The two matters are wholly different don't you see?"

"Of course, but you are stuck and just needed someone to give you a push. If I'd suggested speaking to Alicia you would have dismissed it out of hand but now you have an opportunity. There's so much for you both to discuss. Please, Alicia is waiting. I'm not sure why I'm in here when you should be talking to your wife."

Pursing his lips tightly he sighs through nostrils which are flaring like an enraged bull. He puts his hand to his forehead as if he's had a sudden epiphany.

"Well, I can at least put that matter straight for you. You're here because I had another visit from that Carter-Knowles fellow in your absence."

His voice softens, but my heart still plummets. I can guess what he's about to tell me.

"I take it he wants to see Hannah," I say.

He stares at my daughter who's gurgling away without a care in the world. Her innocence is poignant.

"I'm afraid the situation is rather worse than that, Serena. He wishes to have custody of Hannah if he can and bring her up in a … "more fitting station" were the words he used."

Those words are heavy with sarcasm, and I can picture Dicken enjoying the moment.

150

"He has a strong case, Serena. But I think there's more to it than meets the eye."

I immediately begin to weep without a sound coming from my lips. Dawson passes me his white handkerchief from his pocket as though he had it ready and waiting. I cry silently into the white cloth for it to catch and hold my sorrow.

He's right, Dicken has a sound case, influence and resources at his disposal which I cannot match. He can also point to my deception in forging a new life with Hannah which is evidence that I'm an unfit mother to boot. The nightmare I've predicted since he landed on the doorstep that awful day has now become a reality.

"I'm very sorry to be having this conversation," Dawson says, "he called on Sunday evening sober and polite, unlike the last occasion, asking if he could have a moment of my time. You can imagine my confusion as I was led to believe you were with him attempting to resolve the situation."

I look down at my feet as he clears his throat to go on.

"I think he has regrets over the choices he made not so long ago, and I don't think it's just Hannah he now wants to be part of his life."

No, it can't be. What a preposterous suggestion.

"He can't possibly want us to be together after all that has happened. He didn't want the scandal, the slight on his reputation and because of this I ended up on the streets."

Getting to my feet, I pace the floor as Hannah continues playing, oblivious to the turmoil surrounding her but I know that in a few more years she will be asking questions about her father.

"This is all between the two of you and I'm sure you will have the chance to give him a piece of your mind," he pauses to look up at me, "Serena, I must ask you a very important question, however, if you will indulge my curiosity."

I hold my breath and wait.

"Is his name on Hannah's birth certificate?"

Relief floods through me when I grasp the implication of Dawson's query. I shake my head and as he slumps back in his chair, I almost witness every muscle in his body relaxing. I know now without a doubt how much he has grown to love my little daughter.

"Well then, he can have no claim on her at all. You can rest easy assured that she won't be taken from you and whether you allow him to see her or not is entirely your prerogative."

I raise my eyes to heaven in gratitude and push his huge handkerchief up my sleeve to launder later. I have things to do and so does he.

I pause and look intently at this strange and complex man and will my eyes to convey my affection and gratitude because the words would be so inadequate a response to what he has done for me. I know he understands.

"Well, I must put Hannah to bed, it's past her bedtime. I can only apologise for the upset I've caused but if I were you, I wouldn't waste this chance to turn over a new leaf. I hope in time you find it in your heart to forgive Alicia as I know she's filled with remorse. As for my own future, I need to think about what would be best for all concerned."

Hannah crawls to pull herself up using Dawson's trousers and stands at his knee. Smiling with delight he gently strokes her doughy cheek, so she grins displaying her only two teeth. I enjoy the magical moment but only briefly. I wonder if these little gatherings can continue.

And if indeed it would be right and proper to allow them to do so.

Chapter 24

"All I know Martha is, it's just not fair on you. After all I came to ease your domestic burden, you have barely enough hours in a day as it is."

"Look, life ebbs and flows all the while and you would do well to remember it," she tells me sagely, putting down the iron on the stand at the side of the fire, "Go, have a day to remember, and stop fretting so much."

Alicia bobs her head around the kitchen door in her new winter coat, blueish black like the night sky, and her matching hat finished with a brown feather.

"Our carriage awaits, Serena," she says.

Our relationship is highly irregular and untenable, at least to the outside world and I know this. The lady of the house and the housemaid, what would Moira make of it all.

Kissing Hannah's cheek and then Martha's, I back out of the room, soaking up the little scene of domestic bliss I'm leaving behind.

On this fifth day of November, Guy Fawkes Night, I'm assisted into the carriage wearing my own best dress to accompany Alicia on a shopping trip to Bradford.

Over the last week we've eased into a steadier rhythm at the hall: Dawson comes home from work earlier and after dinner I leave Hannah with him and Alicia for approximately half an hour whilst I help Martha.

Alicia came to see me in my room last night. She couldn't wait to tell me how things are improving between them, and that I've been the subject of much discussion too. Her face was aglow with excitement but

I am filled with trepidation. This is surely the moment when I am asked to make other arrangements.

"I know you will have plenty to say on the matter," she chirrups, speaking twenty to the dozen, "but I would like you to stay at Mallerby as my companion."

She holds up her hand to prevent me from interrupting, "Now hear me out please, before you protest, if you would. Dawson and I owe you a huge debt of gratitude and it would mean a great deal to us to help restore your true status. Dawson has never cared much for convention, and I have reflected on things, shall we say. Gossip will soon fly to the four winds."

Such good news for my future, I should be delighted, but little do they know how uncomfortable it is to watch them together every day. I miss my chats alone with Dawson and pretending I don't have feelings for him with Alicia in the room is becoming difficult to bear. But bear it I must for the time being at least. This problem is mine alone.

Now as agreed, I'm on my way to buy a number of suitable dresses, coats, hats, in fact an entire wardrobe by the sound of it. It sits uneasily but Alicia only thinks this is because I'm too proud to accept.

Her now familiar scent pervades the carriage. It fills it with the smell of meadow flowers though we're in the midst of winter. How pretty she looks; how happy she looks.

"I propose we go to Harriet's for lunch," Alicia says, patting my arm.

I think of my visits there with mama but quickly quash the memory and instead I think of Martha's wise words about the ebb and flow of life. My daughter is my priority, and I must do what I can to secure her future. We are safe at Mallerby Hall under the protection of the Mallerby's.

I listen to the banal chatter of the table next to us in Harriet's and nibble at one of the dainty confectionaries from the stand.

"You looked decidedly awkward choosing your outfits, Serena if you don't mind me saying so. I thought you would be as excited as I am to have some new clothes."

I dab my mouth with my lace napkin and thank the waiter for refilling my teacup.

"I think I've just grown unaccustomed to such fawning attention," I whisper.

Chuckling she says, "You might not have even considered it fawning once. I see there's still a lot of Renee in you, but you must now choose who you wish to be. It is time the pretence was over… for all of us."

I smile and take a sip of tea from my teacup. Class was never even a consideration once as my life was set in stone and I had a 'place'. Today I'm keen to be back at Mallerby Hall. I feel conspicuous, as though I might be recognised and exposed as a fraud at any moment. I once moved in the same circles as Alicia, and I must remember this if I'm to fit back into my new life. Alicia seems to have managed it well enough almost without trying.

I'm content to be bouncing around in the carriage home to Hebden Bridge, delighted to see the hall as we approach. It has become home though oddly I've only just realised this today. Perhaps because I missed Martha as much as the bricks and mortar.

Hello, what's this? Another carriage is in the driveway, and I recognise the driver waiting. Alicia and I exchange glances.

"Oh dear, this is Dicken's carriage," I say as the horses slow.

"Dicken? That man is persistent, I'll give him that. You mustn't panic, Serena, remember what Dawson said—he has no claim."

Martha opens the door to us, her face giving nothing away as she takes our things.

"It's not what you're thinking, Serena, I've been sworn to secrecy but …"

The door opens and there stands Dawson, but he's smiling. I wonder if his smile is fake, and he is trying to forewarn me of the situation.

This is the first time we will all have been together formally in the parlour and I'm thankful for my new and more elegant attire, having kept on a beautiful deep green gown at Alicia's insistence. She told me it complemented the reddish tones of my hair beautifully. I smooth my hair into place now as I follow her into the parlour, glancing over my shoulder at Martha for support. She's nowhere to be seen and I lose my nerve. I'm lightheaded with tension, terrible apprehension about what the outcome of this meeting will be.

Dawson's eyes follow me as I enter the room. Until now he's only seen me in my modest day dress, the one I ran away in, and my working attire and clogs.

He leaves the door ajar saying now, "Serena, I understand our guest will require no introduction."

As he speaks my eyes go to the lady with her back to me on the settee. It can't be, I think and when she turns sideways with her face stretched into the widest smile, I'm still unable to process the scene.

Sitting and waiting patiently for my return to Mallerby Hall has been none other than my dear friend, Rowena.

Oh, joy of joys!

*

"I've heard so much about you, Miss Carter-Knowles," Alicia says taking Rowena's outstretched hand.

My friend's chestnut hair shines in the mid-afternoon sunshine flooding the room.

"Rowena, please," she says, and Alicia inclines her head.

Smiling warmly at each other I'm somehow proud of them both as I look on. These are two special women indeed. Rowena left a gaping hollow in my life, I know it now more than ever.

Dawson moves from the doorway cutting across my thoughts.

"Alicia, I think we should leave our friends to chat a while. I'm sure they have plenty of lost time to make up for," he says.

Strange situations and circumstances are around every corner in this house, I think as they disappear out of the room. For a moment I'm suddenly shy and embarrassed now I'm alone with my old friend. We thought we knew everything there is to know about each other once but now I stand with my hands locked, somehow unable to speak or move.

"Well, Serena my dear we have much to discuss so make haste and come sit by the fire with me."

Her affable tone reminds me why I care so much for Rowena, why I retreated to her house at every given opportunity. I should not have doubted her affection regardless of who her brother might be.

As I sit down, her hand reaches out to touch my arm and I cover it with my own, clinging to it as though she might evaporate at any moment. For a while, we communicate without the need for words.

"Mr Mallerby is a gracious host and he and his wife seem very fond of you," she says.

"I've been fortunate to find such a refuge though life hasn't been straightforward as you know. How did you find me?"

"Dickie told me he'd had someone find you and after a little persuasion disclosed where you were living. Please don't alarm yourself, Serena, I'm certainly not here as his ally. I've missed you, is all and so has mama … very much."

Sweet music to my ears which allows me to settle, my heartbeat slowing. I'm certain Dicken is set to pay me another visit soon. Perhaps she has news.

"But first, may I make a request? I would so love to meet my baby niece if only for a moment," she says.

We are now related by blood, Hannah cementing us as family. The realisation warms me, making me think that perhaps this is how it was always meant to be.

"Of course, wait there, I shan't be long."

We share an affectionate smile before I dash to fetch Hannah. How difficult life has been without my best friend.

Sitting on Martha's knee, Hannah is eating bread and jam, crushing it between her fingers as I dash into the kitchen. I really don't want to lose a second of precious time for my reunion with Rowena. The kettle is steaming on the hob ready for Martha to prepare more refreshments for our guest.

"I can't tell you how happy I am to see Rowena again, Martha," I tell her, "She'd like to be introduced to her niece. Will you come upstairs and meet her too?"

"Ah, look at you, you're a giddy kipper. What a lovely surprise to greet you, this truly has turned out to be a special day after all," she says, passing Hannah into my arms, "I'll bring you both some tea up."

"Martha, you're a treasure," I tell her as I climb the stairs.

How right she is, who would have expected the day to take such a turn when I woke this morning?

Rowena's face sparkles as she clucks and fawns over her baby niece. I think about her parents who are Hannah's grandparents and then my thoughts turn to papa. I realise I've pushed many people to the back of my mind to make it through each day here. I have the constant reminder of Dicken in our daughter's eyes. How I loved his eyes once, now my affections have been seamlessly transferred to her.

"How I wish you would have spoken to me, Serena," she says, tapping Hannah's button nose to make her giggle, "I might have been able to help in some way. I can only imagine how much you have struggled."

"I had to run that day, Weenie, I was so unhappy at home and my … relationship with Dicken meant I could no longer visit Wentworth. Papa was furious with me but mostly I didn't want Moira to be anywhere near my baby, to make her as miserable as she made me. I still think it was the right decision despite the sacrifices it demanded. Mr Mallerby has been my saviour, yes but so too has Martha. She took me under her wing when I was desperate, I owe her a great deal. I think they broke the mould when they made her, she's a very special person."

Right on cue Martha enters the parlour, setting the tea tray on the low table.

"And here she is, Rowena. I've been singing your praises, Martha."

Curtseying, Martha's face glows red at the compliment.

"Ay, well, I thought my ears were burning," she says.

We all laugh together, and I pray it will be the first of many.

"I'm glad Serena found a refuge. It seems your meeting was fate, your friendship meant to be."

She hands a cup and saucer to Rowena, and I notice Martha has smoothed her hair bun with water for the little gathering, the straggling strands tucked neatly behind her ears. My heart melts.

"Sometimes you can't remember your life before someone entered it, and this is how I feel about Serena. She isn't the only one who benefitted from our meeting."

Rowena looks on fondly between us as I smile and drop my head shyly.

"Dada," Hannah says suddenly for the very first time, as clear as a bell for all to hear.

Rowena claps her hand and gasps with delight whilst my smile slips straight from my face.

My round eyes now darting quickly towards Martha, her hanging jaw will no doubt be mirroring my own.

Chapter 25

Even Martha's insistent mutterings will not do anything to sway me this evening.

"This is the least I can do," I tell her buttoning my coat to cover by apron, "There's only Mr Mallerby at this time of day at the factory as Mr Weatherall keeps well out of the way until he leaves. Nobody need ever know if I continue to clean his office and Mr Weatherall wouldn't care if I did. We'll have supper together when I return, Martha as usual. Mr Mallerby said to bring Hannah along so you can get on with the cooking."

He said this, but I can't help thinking he may have ulterior motives.

She blows out her exasperation as I head to the back door. Time is getting on and I must go.

"Looks like I've little choice in the matter," she touches my shoulder gently, "you've a heart as pure as gold you know lass."

I plant a kiss clumsily on her cheek before I shunt Hannah's perambulator down the back steps with expert ease. Turning, I wave to Martha as I head towards the woodland path. She waves back, watching us until we disappear.

I'm still walking on air after Rowena's unexpected visit. Tucking the blankets tightly under Hannah's chin against the evening air, she's wide awake and responsive making me glad already of our new little arrangement.

Rowena said Dicken hasn't told their parents which surprises me. I'm relieved but Hannah is their grandchild after all. If Dicken's parents find out, then they're sure to tell papa where I am. The shame of encountering my father again sickens me.

"Does Anabelle know about Hannah yet, Weenie?" I asked.

"No, not yet. I'm the only one he's told for the time being, but he does seem keen to have his daughter in his life," she paused, "he's asked me to tell you he's made a terrible mistake. He still loves you, Serena, although I imagine you don't feel the same after all that's happened. I think it's been a case of not knowing how he truly felt about you until you were gone."

Despite Dawson's suspicions about Dicken's motives, Rowena took me by surprise. I had convinced myself Dicken only had eyes on his daughter. Now our time together on the moors seems so shallow, frivolous even though how could I know it then? Dicken is immature, half the man Dawson is, and I'm prepared to live without love until I meet someone who has Dawson's sincerity and integrity. I can't possibly settle for anything less now I know the difference.

But I knew I must keep my thoughts about Rowena's brother to myself. I must keep my cards close to my chest.

"I admit his about turn has taken me unawares. I thought he cared about Anabelle; they've only been married two minutes after all."

Tutting, Rowena rolled her eyes.

"Anabelle is a millstone around his neck," she said, her nose wrinkling with distaste, "if you recall all she thinks about is money and status the same as her parents. Her dowry apparently was less impressive than he was led to believe."

Oh, I see, so it was all about the money. It transpires I had a lucky escape for yet another reason.

Rowena stayed for supper, providing her usual jolly company for the Mallerby's, and we watched the impressive firework displays of the village on the back lawn with a glass of sherry. I didn't want her to leave, but she said she hoped it would be acceptable for her to visit again. Of course, was the resounding answer.

But she wouldn't be pressed on Dicken's plan of action, telling me she thought he would just like to see Hannah from time to time the same as she. Perhaps he'd had time to reconsider after his chat with Dawson.

It was indeed a splendid and unexpected Guy Fawkes's Night.

There's a frost settling on the boggy pathway this evening, making it treacherous underfoot. I step gingerly onto the yard, thankful now to finally arrive at the factory in one piece. Perhaps it would be best not to use the shortcut in wintertime.

Startled by the snap of twig in the silence, I turn quickly around, only to see a blackness descending quickly.

It descends too quickly to see what or who causes me to tumble to the ground.

There isn't even time for me to let out a scream.

*

"Don't even think about getting up, missy."

I hear Martha's voice commanding me as if from another room, though I see her face clearly in front of me, her hand on my shoulder. I slowly realise I'm lying in my bed, my head split by a headache.

As she places a cup to my lips, I take the water gratefully then lie back on the pillows, exhausted by the simple act.

"Why am I here, Martha? What has happened. The last thing I recall is being on the path near the factory and now I'm lying here."

She perches on the bed, smoothing the hair away from my forehead in a gesture so motherly. Her eyes won't meet mine.

"Now, don't fret Little Robin, you've had a bump to the head, and you were lying on the freezing ground for some time before Mr Weatherall found you and raised the alarm."

"How did I get home?"

She raises her eyebrows and smiles without teeth.

"Now thereby hangs a tale. The master bounced into the house with you in his arms, startling the living daylights out of the rest of us. Before we knew it you were up here on the bed with him barking the order for the doctor to be summoned immediately. I thought the worse for a while, we all did. What a to do we've had. By, it's good to have you back with us again, Serena."

"How long have I been here?"

"Since yesterday," she sighs, "you've been in and out of consciousness all this time though I could tell you weren't really back with us when you woke afore. One more hour of it and you were going to have to go to the infirmary in Halifax the doctor said," she tells me, standing, "I'll go fetch you a drop of broth, I imagine you're famished."

Grabbing hold of Martha's sleeve, I pull her back to sitting down. I must stop her from leaving, she must tell me why I'm in such a state.

"Serena, you're awake. I can't tell you how pleased I am," Alicia says crossing the room to sit on the other side of the bed. Her face, bearing a smile I know is fake, hovers above me, unnervingly. I know I

165

should feel wrapped in a cocoon of safety as two hands hold mine, one veined and reddened the other pale and refined, both equally trying to provide comfort. But this does nothing to settle me.

"Please, I'd like to see Hannah, and I must know what happened," I say.

I see an exchange of anxious glances. My eyes flip between both their faces as I wait for an answer too slow in coming.

"Now, you must get well and not worry, Hannah is having a little nap," Martha says.

"Martha, I'm fast losing my manners. Nap or no nap, I would be grateful if you could tell me what has happened to us or I shall jump out of bed this instant and go see for myself."

Dropping my hand, she sits up clearly too taken aback to find the words.

"Serena, I'm afraid you've taken a blow to the head. You were struck by someone," Alicia says, stepping in to explain on her behalf.

"Struck?" I ask.

Martha sighs saying, "Look, I think it better if we speak plainly, this agitation can't be helping her recovery. Serena, I'm sorry to say we believe Mr Dicken has taken Hannah."

Taken Hannah, what on earth can she mean?

"But the master has everything in hand, so she'll be back home before you know it," Martha quickly carries on, seeing the effect her explanation is having on me.

Her words finally sinking in, I sit bolt upright.

"Taken her where?"

Patting my hand, I snatch it away as if burned. She folds her hands in her lap, her chest heaving.

"Dawson is looking into the matter, but rest assured he shan't have her long, not if we have anything to do with it," Alicia says.

Looking into the matter—I've heard enough. I'm up and out of bed like a woman possessed. If they think they will deter me from getting out of this house, they don't know me at all. They don't know any mother.

Heading to the bathroom I grab my clothes on the way as they both stand looking on helplessly from the side of my empty bed.

I have a sudden realisation now as I lock the bathroom door: neither of them could possibly know how I feel at this moment as sadly neither of them has been blessed enough to become a mother.

I want to cry. I want to cry for too many reasons choking me all at once.

Chapter 26

I bounce past a startled Miss Rutland who jumps up from her desk. She utters some sort of objection which I completely ignore.

She's not quick enough to waylay me so I'm met with an equally startled Dawson Mallerby as I barge open his office door. Knocking doesn't even enter my head.

"Serena, what on earth are you doing out of bed!" he exclaims, rushing from his seat to my side.

As he extends his hand, I push it away and he takes a step backwards.

"Alright, alright, I see you know about Hannah," he says pointing to a chair, "I only ask you to sit a moment so I can acquaint you with the situation."

It's only now I notice another person in the room. The person is standing with an alarmed expression, his mouth gaping as he looks between us.

Dawson makes his introductions as he ushers me towards a seat.

"Serena, this is Mr Barker. He's a private detective whom I've taken the liberty of hiring on your behalf whilst you have been incapacitated. Please …" he extends his arm once more to the chair to encourage me to sit down.

I submit finally though I'd prefer to stand. When both men now follow suit and sit down, I come to my senses a little, feeling quite rude.

"I'm sure you will forgive my impolite entrance under the circumstances, but I apologise nonetheless."

"Good afternoon, Miss Wilton-Robbins, I'm sorry to be meeting you under those difficult circumstances," Mr Barker says.

Dawson's look of pity makes me avert my eyes. I'm sure I look a frightful mess, but so be it, a frightful mess is what I am at this time. The wave comes again—Hannah my darling, where are you?

"Well, I had no option but to seek assistance as I drew a blank when I spoke to Carter-Knowles about Hannah's whereabouts. I was at risk of losing my temper and making a terrible situation worse so I'm hoping Mr Barker's discreet enquiries may help us," Dawson says.

He slides from his desk to squat and wrap a hand around my arm then pat it gently. I don't pull away even though Mr Barker's eyes are upon us. This is the least of my worries and Dawson will not care about him looking at us one jot.

"You've spoken to Dicken," I say with surprise.

"Yes, it was the first thing I did once it became clear Hannah had gone. I telephoned Wentworth but he dismissed any knowledge of what has happened to Hannah.

"I didn't believe him and was going to involve the police, but Alicia thought a private detective would be your preferred line of enquiry."

I'm not sure if discretion is paramount any longer, but at least for the time being Mr Barker will be able to give my missing daughter his undivided attention. It doesn't take a genius to realise who is at the heart of it.

"Well, I'll be on my way now, Mr Mallerby," Mr Barker says then inclines his head my way, "Miss Wilton-Robbins. I will keep you informed of any progress with the … the situation."

I barely acknowledge his words as he leaves us.

169

I look at Dawson's weary face, his hair raked with agitation, his green eyes sunken, sallow like the murky depths of the seabed. I doubt he will have slept the whole time I've been sleeping. He will have been pushing himself to the limit in my absence because he loves my baby daughter, I know this if nothing else.

"Hannah has been gone for well over a day, Dawson, she could be anywhere by now. I couldn't even put it past Dicken to take her out of the county," I say my voice rising steadily with panic at the realisation.

He crouches to hold both my hands in his, squeezing them in an effort to calm me.

"Rest assured, Serena, if she were in Timbuktu, I will find her. I will not stop until I do."

Whether he can, remains to be seen but I've no doubt it won't be for the want of trying.

"I want to help," I say raising my hand, "please don't try and stop me because I will lose my mind at home waiting all day. I must be useful, Dawson. I must."

I'm becoming hysterical, he must listen to me.

Standing to his full height he looks down at me, then drops his head back and sighs knowing he is beaten. He knows I will flee the house if he tries to deter me.

"Well then, all I ask is we have the doctor visit you at home today and then, after a good night's sleep, you can help tomorrow …if he thinks you fit enough. You'll not be any use if you're still unwell and you must think of Hannah," he pauses, "have faith Serena, Mr Barker comes highly recommended and may even have found her by the time you wake tomorrow such is his reputation."

I give a small nod to his request. He's right of course.

But as he pulls me from my seat to place my arm in his to walk past Miss Routledge and a hundred clog-makers on the way to his carriage and home, I can't help but think that in some cases and for some people, tomorrow simply never comes.

*

The clock has only just struck six this November morning and I've already begun my day in earnest.

I asked Martha to send a telegram to Rowena yesterday saying I must speak with her as a matter of urgency. I didn't want to call for fear of raising suspicions at Wentworth. She has agreed to come to the hall as requested. I've been wondering since if she knows about Hannah or if Dicken has kept her in the dark. Soon, all will be revealed.

The doctor said I must rest but it was out of the question. A white lie is for the best I consoled myself after he left. I wanted so badly to leave with him as my room was like a cage the whole day as I paced and fretted.

However, by then I had the good sense to realise I must tread very carefully if I am to find my daughter quickly.

Dawson's telephone call to Wentworth will have alerted Dicken that we are on to him, and I wonder what he will do next. He must know I would never give Hannah up, never. How does he think he will get away with this without any repercussions. But it's clear to me his mind must be unhinged and he has now risked all.

Last evening Mr Slater knocked on my door to tell me Mr & Mrs Mallerby would like me to dine with them should I feel well enough. By then I was beside myself, keen to escape the confines of my cage.

We sat at the dining table. My previous discomfort at our strange fellowship gone and replaced only with thoughts of Hannah.

"We haven't been entirely honest about what happened that evening," Alicia said, as if making polite dinner table conversation.

I look up from my untouched plate with a start, wondering what new misery will emerge.

"As Dawson described, he did indeed telephone Wentworth, but the conversation didn't end with a denial by Carter-Knowles as we led you to believe.

My expression must now clearly bely my sense of hurt that they would keep such details from me.

"Please, you must understand at that point you were gravely ill," she offers in defence.

I know this is reasonable but I'm still seething with them.

"Dawson wasn't convinced as you know so he told Carter-Knowles that if he did not meet him by seven o'clock the following morning in his office at the factory, he would be receiving a visit at Wentworth or his place of work. At that stage Dawson mistakenly thought Hannah was nearby and would be home with us the following day. As Anabelle knows nothing of Hannah's existence as yet, Dawson was banking on this forcing his hand and Dawson was proved correct. Carter-Knowles was keen to avoid any unpleasantness."

Bless Alicia, she's well ahead of the game and reads the situation so well. She's grown fond of

Hannah during the time they've spent together, and I know both she and Dawson look forward to their evening play sessions. My little daughter lives in a very avantgarde but very loving environment. She must return to it soon.

"The following morning Carter-Knowles slunk into the building like the weasel he is, well before seven. The last thing he wants is a scandal."

Dawson put his fork down as Alicia and I looked at him.

"I didn't intend to refer to you and Hannah as a scandal; that was an unfortunate turn of phrase and I apologise."

"No apology necessary, that wasn't what I was thinking at all," I said.

I wasn't, I only wanted him to continue with his story so I could dissect the information and perhaps deduce a clue to where Hannah might be. I had regained some equilibrium then and could feel my tension easing.

Dawson continued the story: "So, dispensing with pleasantries I asked him the obvious question only to be told he had no idea where Hannah was and even if he did, it was none of my business. Technically he was right of course but I still had to hold on to every ounce of self-control. I asked him if he would tell you where she is should you wake. This shook him a little presumably because he clearly had no idea how ill you were.

"Do you mean to say that Serena is still unconscious?" he asked, his expression giving away his shock at finding out otherwise and confirming my suspicions that he was the culprit. I told him you had been in and out of consciousness but if anything should happen, he would be charged with murder or at least an accomplice to murder as I doubt that he was the person who struck the blow. Then, appealing to his better nature—though I'm not sure such a man has one—I said I knew you would be glad to arrange a meeting to discuss your daughter's future and such extreme measures were uncalled for.

His response to this was that he refused to sit around waiting for a visit from his own daughter. That is even if you, Serena should deign to allow him the opportunity."

Dawson shook his head at the memory and took a huge gulp of wine. He detests the man; I could see it yet who could blame him?

"You know, perhaps he's right, I would have found it difficult to allow him any access to Hannah," I said.

Hindsight is a wonderful thing. I could never have predicted Dicken would go to such lengths.

"Regardless, Serena, he told me he would be making his own enquiries as to where Hannah might have been taken. I'm afraid we're dealing with a stubborn and manipulative individual. The man is fully aware we're as keen as he is to prevent all this becoming common knowledge. For the moment he has us over a barrel which is why I've secured the services of Mr Barker."

My eyes dropped to the uneaten food on my plate, and I shivered as a chill ran up my back. Taking a small sip of wine, the warmth was a comfort as it slid down my throat and into my stomach. Alicia gave me a small smile and I could have wept.

"I've asked Rowena to call tomorrow. I don't think she will betray our trust and if anyone can shed light on the matter it will be her," I said.

"I think that's a very good idea," Alicia said, her face etched with compassion.

All the time we were dining I thought of Mr Barker trying to find Hannah, of my beautiful little girl being held in goodness knows what surroundings and by strangers.

Thanking the Mallerby's for their hospitality, I left them at just past nine o'clock.

I returned to my empty room and placed a log on the fire as I always did last thing at night. I undressed and wandered over to the bed as though asleep already even though sleep would not come all night.

I climbed into bed and pulled up the freezing sheets thinking that a scandal was becoming less and less of a concern every hour which passed without my daughter with me.

Let me atone for my sins if this is what they are, I thought, let me stand and face the crowds. I have nothing to be ashamed of, I've learned this now.

And then in the silent darkness of Mallerby Hall I cried into my pillow until hours later the clock struck five to finally announce it was time to face the day ahead and make every last second of it count towards accomplishing my mission.

Chapter 27

This morning I feel as though I'm the lady in residence of Mallerby Hall as I await Rowena's arrival. I'm unable to sit still so I stand and moon out of the window instead, twirling a curl at the side of my ear manically. The rain splatters against the glass only heightening my sense of misery.

Alicia offered to join us, but I think this a conversation best left to the two of us, so she has gone out in the carriage to run errands. I was tempted to accept her kind offer of support, but the last thing I want is for Rowena to feel intimidated, it's important she tells me everything she knows and what is happening at Wentworth.

I see Rowena's carriage approach the hall and her man help her down then shelter her under a huge umbrella to the entrance. Oh, at last, I think. Unable to wait a second longer, I rush to open the drawing room door myself before Mr Slater has even had time to help Rowena out of her coat. Martha has already brought up our tea which she placed on a trivet by the fire to keep warm.

Rowena bustles my way, kissing my cheek lightly before she sits down.

"I've been worried sick, Serena. What on earth has happened that is so pressing?" she asks, inadvertently answering the question burning through my mind. Thank goodness my friend is also in the dark, I think. But then the relief is quickly replaced by frustration my meeting with her this morning may be a complete waste of precious time.

There is no way to prepare her for the shock, I must just get on with it. Our tea goes untouched as I update her on the dreadful state of affairs. Perhaps she can at least share what she knows of Dicken's activities and behaviour.

Her expression of incredulity mounts with each word, her eyes growing ever wider until she finally gets to her feet, distress making it impossible for her to sit still.

"Surely, you're mistaken, Serena. Dicken would never do such a thing; forgive me but I find it hurtful you could even suggest he might. My brother is many things and I know the situation between you is strained…but a common criminal… have you taken leave of your senses?"

My palm presses the base of my throat.

"Strained is perhaps under-stating matters," I say, trying my best to restrain the irritation I feel, "I understand how this must be a shock for you Rowena and I'm so sorry, but there was no easy way to break the news. Believe me I wish Hannah was still with me and Dicken was not under suspicion."

She paces the floor for several minutes and I allow her the time to digest the revelation. Stopping at the window she stares onto the wet grounds for a second and then turns to face me directly.

"If he has snatched Hannah, if indeed he has, what does he hope to achieve? Where would he take her?" she asks.

She's clearly finding it difficult to see her brother in such a light and only two days ago I would have felt exactly the same.

"Well, this is the question; we have no idea, but we have a person making enquiries on our behalf," I say.

She slumps back into her chair like a ragdoll and stares through the portrait of Dawson in the alcove.

"So, I'm here because you need my help," she says sullenly.

I nod, my eyes stinging.

"I'm desperate, Rowena, I wouldn't ask otherwise but I wonder if he's taken her further afield. You must understand I'm at risk of never seeing my baby again."

Rowena is a different kettle of fish to her brother altogether, I know this if nothing else. Appealing to her better nature will not fall on deaf ears as it did with Dicken.

"Well then," she sighs, "as unbelievable as all this seems you must tell me exactly what you know. Start at the very beginning and leave nothing out."

"My information is limited but I'm due to see Mr Barker shortly and I'm hoping he at least has made some progress."

"I'll come with you," she says.

Such a generous gesture to make, I'm touched. This is an indication she wants to help despite her misgivings.

"I can't thank you enough," I say.

"Serena, you and I are family. If Dicken is behind this, and I confess I can't help but still have my doubts, but if he is, we must find her. I must make him see sense."

Oh, the relief, she has no idea. I should have had faith my friend would come to my aid. With Rowena's support there is still hope, I think.

At three o'clock on the dot Mr Barker arrives at Dawson's office and is greeted by a veritable committee: Dawson, Alicia, Rowena and me. He takes the sight of our ensemble in his professional stride, barely batting an eye as he sits down to join us. Extra chairs have been brought into the office.

Dawson introduces Rowena advising that she is Dicken's sister but is here to help us in any capacity she can, and she can be trusted implicitly.

"I see, well I think that will be very helpful to my investigation. I'm sure you understand I must speak frankly," Mr Barker says, "unfortunately, I've been following your brother all day, but there's little to report. I think he suspects he is being followed and so he is being very careful."

"Indeed, assuming he is the culprit," Rowena interjects.

Mr Barker strokes his silver moustache absentmindedly then retrieves a small and somewhat worn leather-bound notebook from the pocket of his raincoat and proceeds to read aloud an itinerary of movements, locations and times. The mundane minutiae of Dicken's day.

"Nothing of note there," he concludes "however he remains the main suspect; he has means and motive, and therefore must remain the focus of the investigation."

Turning to Rowena he asks, "Do you know of any friends he might have involved?"

Of course, Timothy, I think as Rowena looks hesitant. She glances in my direction unsure if she should disclose the name. If she doesn't, sadly she knows I will. She must know this.

"Well, there's a Timothy Kendal and another friend from his university days, Thomas Forbes. I think Timothy can be taken out of the frame as I spend a substantial amount of my time with him. We are engaged to be married."

Rowena stands and I realise now this is her default position when anxious.

"I also must speak frankly, Mr Barker. I can't think my brother would stoop to such a level. He doesn't even know his daughter. I do hope you will maintain the utmost discretion as you go about your enquiries, particularly as you do not have any proof as yet, he is involved."

Dawson interjects telling Rowena of the conversation he had with Dicken on the day after Hannah was abducted. She sits down and sighs and I see it as a sign she is beginning to accept what she's being told. I close my eyes briefly; we might have his sister on our side finally.

"What do you consider to be the best course of action now, Mr Barker?" Alicia asks, "Should Rowena speak to her brother, try to make him see sense perhaps?"

Holding up his hand, Mr Barker shakes his head saying, "No, I think it best to keep that powder dry for the time being. I understand this will be difficult for you, Miss Carter-Knowles but the less your brother knows the better. I hope you understand. Also, I must add that I know you have your doubts about your brother but in my experience, it is often the case in these matters that the culprit's family and friends were kept completely in the dark."

"So, I'm to pretend nothing has happened; is this your suggestion?"

Rowena looks my way, shaking her head at the thought.

"I think it best, for the time being at least. I hope not for too long."

Mr Barker turns to me, "I hate to mention this, Miss Wilton-Robbins but it may be necessary for you to try and meet Mr Carter-Knowles at some point. Of course, I won't ask this of you unless I think it absolutely necessary you understand."

He looks pained to be saying the words.

And while Dawson is telling Mr Barker this idea would simply be out of the question, I'm sitting quietly thinking it will be my pleasure to meet that man.

The man who can seek to deny it all he wishes but who I feel certain is undoubtedly at the heart of this misery.

Chapter 28

It's purely because I am a mother.

I remind myself constantly of this because dark, disturbing thoughts make me ashamed and bold in equal measure. My only thought is how to find my daughter, nothing else and I'm horrified by the lengths I'm considering going to.

Mr Barker appears to have no sense of urgency, plodding from one move to the next. I need action; I must take action. Three days is too long a time for any mother to suffer to such a degree.

I've considered going to the police station many times. To hell with my whereabouts and my situation being exposed, I think, to hell with the shame on the family. My daughter is more important than anything.

However, none of us think Dicken would let Hannah come to any harm. If he did it would be the gallows for him. No, he just wants to take revenge on me. I still can't accept that he simply wants to be part of his daughter's life.

Dawson assures me Mr Barker has an excellent track record and is the person to bring my daughter home and counsels that a softly, softly approach rather than a police investigation is less likely to make Dicken reckless and unpredictable. I'm trying my utmost to trust his judgement. At least the private investigator is devoting his full focus to the cause which would not be the case with the police.

I hear horse's hooves clattering into the courtyard and dash to the kitchen window, knowing full well before the carriage comes into view that Dawson has arrived. He must have news. Alicia, Mr Slater, Martha, and I rush to the front door from our respective rooms of the house to greet him without a word spoken between us.

Stepping back, he's surprised by the welcoming committee in the hallway. He strides past Mr Slater, not even taking off his coat, only throwing his hat on the table. He misses the mark but doesn't notice.

"What is it? Have you found her?" I ask, my heart pounding, my mouth dry as a desert.

His face gives nothing away as he puts both hands on my arms.

"Barker has a lead, yes. It seems that Carter-Knowles' friend Thomas Forbes has moved, and Barker bribed a fellow frequenter at the village inn who was a little worse for wear to disclose where he now lives. Barker thinks it too much of a coincidence for him to have left so suddenly."

"As do I," I say, removing myself from his hold to turn and seek confirmation from Alicia and Martha, who are both nodding in agreement.

"What can be done?" I ask with more than a hint of impatience.

"Come, let us adjourn to the drawing room," Dawson says as Alicia and I follow him like the Pied Piper down the hallway. Slater asks if drinks are required and Dawson nods. Martha says she will bring tea for the ladies.

He flings his long coat onto the back of his chair and remains standing as we all perch on our seats around him.

"Obviously, Barker needs to keep tabs on Forbes but Serena we must remain patient. It may take a day or two to smoke him out and we can't afford to lose such a lead, do you understand what I'm saying to you?"

His anxious eyes unsettle me as I nod solemnly, accepting the sense of his argument. He's worried I might take matters into my own hands and ruin everything.

It had seemed a breakthrough at the time but when after three days we discover that Forbes's relocation had nothing to do with Hannah, but rather it was about some dispute over rent, I know without doubt what must be done next.

*

"Now where pray tell do you think you're going?"

Stopping mid step, I whip my head to stare straight into the quizzical eyes of Dawson Mallerby. His chair is positioned to give him a clear view of the hallway and one lower leg is placed at a ninety-degree angle over the other thigh. He's been sitting there on watch all night by the look of him.

I put down my bag silently onto the tiles so as not to wake the household then walk into the room and close the door quietly. I'm in my outerwear including hat and I stay holding onto the handle because I shan't be staying long no matter what he has to say. I rise to my full height and lift my chin to prepare for battle.

"You'll not stop me, Dawson. I'm going to Wentworth to see Anabelle. I feel as though I'm buried alive in this house. She will need to know one way or another and now is the time."

Dropping his leg, he shuffles to the edge of his seat, his eyes never leaving mine. My stance droops slightly at the silent treatment.

"I'm sorry, but I must take the first train. I need to leave before Martha wakes and tries to talk me out of it. I've written her a note."

Yet still he doesn't speak.

"I'll be on my way then," I say turning the door handle.

As he stands and walks the few steps between us, I'm not the least bit intimidated.

Taking my hand, he plants me in his vacated seat.

"If you are set on this course of action, and I can plainly see you are, then at least wait a moment whilst I rouse Bailey to take us to the station. Bailey can inform Martha so they're not worried about us. However, I have to say I think you are wasting time in visiting Anabelle. I have a better idea which I can explain in the carriage if you'll allow me. If I'm wrong, we can revert to your original plan. Do you agree?"

I look down at my feet.

"Yes, this is acceptable … and thank you," I say.

Touching my cheek, so briefly and softly I wonder if I imagined it, he sweeps from the room.

"I was certain you would try to talk me out of it," I say when we're settled in the carriage on our way to the station.

My heart is dancing with love for this man. He gives a wry smile.

"I know better by now than to stand in the way of a mother who is losing her mind with worry. I had a feeling you might run in the night, so I made sure I was ready and waiting if it happened. To be perfectly frank I was considering what course of action to take myself today now Barker has hit a dead end."

I clear my throat.

"Did Alicia not wonder where you were?" I ask.

Looking out of the window into the darkness of the winter morning he shifts in his seat.

"She would be neither aware nor unaware of my absence as presently we do not share a bedroom."

I think how to change the subject swiftly and follow his gaze out of the window, my face burning.

"It won't be long before Dicken leaves for work," I say, stating the obvious but pleased to have found a way to divert the conversation.

"If we draw a blank with him again, would you like me to come to the house with you to see his wife?" he asks.

"Thank you but no, I think it would be best if I went alone."

His presence would be a comfort, but this again is a conversation to be had woman to woman. I wonder where to begin such a conversation and decide transparency will be better all round in the long run. Hiding our indiscretion from Dicken's wife now comes a poor second to finding my daughter.

"If you have feelings for Carter-Knowles, you should tell him. This could be your saving grace, Serena. I imagine you have already considered this?"

It's not a valid option for so many reasons but most importantly, I do not have feelings for Dicken any longer, and for what he has done to Hannah, I now detest the man with a passion. Yet I have considered lying about this. A new plan has been formulating, one which under ordinary circumstances I would be ashamed of but needs must in this instance, I think, and I wasn't the one who put us in this dreadful situation.

I don't speak of this with Dawson and I'm thankful he doesn't push for an answer.

At fifteen minutes past eight Dawson and I find ourselves waiting close to Dicken's workplace to catch him on his way to work. Dawson looks out of the window as each carriage approaches the clearing then shakes his head when we're disappointed.

Finally turning towards me, he pats my hand then I watch him dismounting the carriage at speed. He flags down a carriage coming in the opposite direction and I hear the horses steadily coming to a halt then grunt and whinny as they settle. Muffled voices drift my way as I sit hands knotted pensively in the cold carriage, the blanket providing little comfort.

I'm startled when the carriage door opens suddenly, and I see Dicken for the first time since he descended on Mallerby Hall. I look at the face of the man whom I once thought was the love of my life, now the father of my child. I'm unsettled by the sight of him. What will he say? Too many emotions hurtle my way to process, and I scrabble in my bag for a handkerchief.

Dicken climbs in and slams the door leaving us alone but for Bailey atop the carriage. Where is Dawson I wonder and as an afterthought, I think I will bang on the roof should I require assistance. The last time I was alone with Dicken was the day I told him he was to be a father. My obvious distress clearly gives him cause for alarm.

"Serena, my love, please don't concern yourself, I'm here to help," he gabbles, "I've been a selfish fool and much more that isn't fit for a lady to hear, but that discussion is for another time. All that matters now is that we find our daughter; I thought you would have found her by now. I was planning to come and see you later today to speak with you about my intentions and I hoped you would listen to what I had to say."

What is this change of demeanour? I don't trust it.

"Dicken, let me make myself clear; I care nothing of my reputation any longer let alone your own. We must go to the police. This has gone on long enough and I'm unable to suffer it a moment longer. You shouldn't want me to suffer like this."

My voice is raised, and he puts his hand on my arm attempting to calm me. I can't be calmed; I only sit taking great gulps of air. I'm suffocating but I must stay and have this difficult discussion for the time being at least. I must make him see sense.

"If you truly wish to make amends, the first thing you can do is support me and stop these pathetic denials. It is wicked and if you truly wanted to be a real father to Hannah then she is all you would care about right now, ensuring she is returned to her mother and the people who love her."

The words keep tumbling out and, in my desperation to make him see my point of view, before I can stop them, I say it:

"The situation is far bigger than the two of us, our daughter is my only priority and if we are to have any chance you must start to be a father this very moment."

His eyes clouding, I know I've awakened something in him for the first time. It's only a pity the point had to be hammered home for him.

He turns to grab both my forearms with the look of a haunted man.

"You are right of course, Serena. I'm sorry I've been thinking only of myself. But you must know that I am as much in the dark about Hannah's whereabouts as you are. I swear it."

There is a desperate look in his eyes now which catches the light from the streetlamp, making him look like a hunted animal.

And suddenly I know.

I know that he is telling the truth.

Burying my face into my handkerchief, I weep softly on and on like I might never stop.

My daughter is more out of my reach than she ever was.

All hope is now lost.

Chapter 29

The sound of Dicken's voice has faded behind the sound of my own heart breaking. I hear only the wretched sound of my own sobs and see only blackness. There is no way out of this purgatory.

We were so certain Dicken had taken Hannah. It seemed so straightforward as he had a clear reason to, however misguided. But the prospect that some stranger has taken her is a nightmare of wholly different proportions. I don't know if I can survive this.

A man's voice appears nearer and slowly the velvet drapes at the carriage windows come into focus.

"Come Serena, Serena … you can't break now, Hannah needs you," Dicken says, displaying the tenderness that won me over on our moorland trysts.

I look his way, still dazed and mutter, "You know there is no option now. We must inform the police," and realise I'm saying it to myself as much as to him.

This time there is no objection or debate.

"Of course, I only ask that we forestall perhaps one or two hours to allow me to speak to Anabelle and my parents."

He drops my arms to slump in his seat, perhaps seeing my hesitation.

"Please, I owe them an explanation at least. I can't let them find out second hand, it would be too cruel."

As panicked as I am at the thought of any delay however brief, I have a stirring of pride towards him. This is the action of a man and not a spoiled little boy. When I touch his hand, he takes both my own in his and I drop my head on his shoulder. He finally understands and we're joined as one for the sake of our baby. Relief washes over me.

We agree to meet later in the morning at the town hall in Huddersfield and go from there to the police station together. It will be a long morning, but he's at least trying to do the right thing as all this will come as a shock to his family. Anabelle and his parents are going to have their world turned upside down and it's only right they should be forewarned. I console myself that at this moment I would have still been talking to Anabelle and I doubt any further in my search. Now I will have his support going forward.

After Dicken leaves Dawson returns, the damp morning mist still clinging to his coat.

"It isn't Dicken, I'm certain of it," I say.

He looks tired, his face drawn and tight. I want to touch it, but I can't.

"Are you absolutely certain he's telling you the truth? You must be certain, Serena."

I nod.

Dropping his head, he looks at his hands saying, "I'm glad he's stepping up to his responsibilities for her sake … and for yours."

The note of sadness in his voice upsets me. Perhaps he thinks he might lose the child who has become so dear to him. A child he has protected and cared for so well. I grip his gloved hand and his fingers curl around mine.

"Dawson, you have my word that whatever happens once I find my daughter you will always, always be part of her life. You took us into your home when I had nothing, no one and I will never forget it. You and Martha, even Mr Slater and now Alicia, we have become almost like a little family, joined by the love of my daughter, and I could never walk away and leave you all behind. It would not be in her best interests or mine, believe me."

Raising his head, the pain is too much to ignore, and I reach to touch his cheek, the desolation which has always been there remaining still. How unhappy this man is for a myriad of reasons.

"Come," he says with a brittle smile, "let us get out of this cold morning air and take some refreshment. Even if we only pretend to eat at least we shall be warm whilst we wait."

Our hands remain entwined the whole journey into town.

At eleven o'clock we descend on the town hall a few minutes early surprised to discover Dicken is already there, pacing the cobbles as he waits. Something tells me even before he sees us that he has news and as we step from the carriage, I rush ahead of Dawson to find out what it can be, his anxious look confirming my suspicions.

"What is it, Dicken?" I ask in a panicked voice.

He stops pacing to face us, his mouth set and I sense our plans have changed yet again. I know more of this man than I realised.

"Serena, Mallerby," Dicken says, "I don't quite know how to say this, but there is no need for us to involve the police after all."

We both stare at him, the apprehension tightening my throat almost to the point of being unable to swallow air. I can't believe he has gone back on everything he swore to me only a few hours ago. My face set like granite, I wait for his explanation.

"After we spoke, I have been thinking all morning, and I have a strong suspicion as to Hannah's whereabouts."

Oh, thank heavens, Dicken I think, as both men rush to my aid when my legs buckle, preventing me from a fall.

Is it too much to ask that this living nightmare could finally be over?

*

I was quickly bundled back into our carriage, and it was agreed that we would adjourn to Dawson's office at Millthwaite's. I began to allow myself the solace of thinking my beloved Hannah might soon be home with me.

Dawson sent a telegram to Mr Barker's office before we left Huddersfield asking him to join us, though I thought his presence unnecessary and the delay in sending the telegram a waste of our valuable time. I told him as much.

"Serena, perhaps Mr Barker may have information of his own which will confirm or deny Dicken's suspicions."

I sigh and sit back in the seat of the carriage with resignation.

"Fine," I say looking straight ahead before he dashes away.

Miss Rutland serves refreshments to the gentlemen and leaves my cup untouched. However, Dawson soon reminds her of what I know was an intentional oversight. Leaving the room, her bad manners exposed, she can't help herself and gives me a withering look. I barely notice; I have bigger fish to fry than this petty woman.

Mr Barker eventually arrives and he leans forward with his forearms resting on his knees to listen intently to Dicken's account.

"I left my wife to go over to Wentworth House, my parent's home having decided to tell my parent's first," he says for Mr Barker's benefit, "of course at that time of the morning only my mother was home; ordinarily, I would have wanted to tell them together, but time was of the essence. You can imagine how difficult it was to broach the subject and I expected my mother to be shocked. However, she was nowhere near as horrified as I thought. Her odd reaction immediately raised my suspicion, it was so out of character, but I left thinking I might be misreading the situation. It wouldn't be the first time," he added, giving me a slight smile that didn't match the sorrowful look in his eyes.

"I left my mother quicker than I would have liked to go see my father at his office. This too I knew was inappropriate, but again I had no alternative. My father is a strong, stoic man, a man to admire and I do. This was somehow the hardest of the three conversations. As a son, to disappoint one's father is a bitter pill to swallow."

Shaking his head he looks my way, but I'm unable to react only wanting him to get to the point.

"He looked as though he might break down rather than be angry or disappointed, but he recovered himself quickly. This too was out of character, and I left with the oddest of sensations.

He pauses to look at all three of us in turn.

"I suspect my parents have something to do with Hannah's disappearance."

His parents … what is he thinking?

"So, you've got us here because of some ridiculous hunch!" Dawson barks, "We have delayed going to the police and raised Serena's hopes only to have them dashed over your strange feelings. You could have told us this in Huddersfield. I knew you couldn't be trusted. Serena, be done with this liar once and for all."

His voice is brittle with contempt, but I have my own thoughts on the matter.

"Perhaps you might have point," I say as Dawson continues huffing and muttering under his breath as I'm speaking.

"As Dicken was talking, I was thinking along those lines. Rowena knows about Hannah because you told her Dicken. She may have let it slip in a conversation with her parents and illegitimate or not, Hannah is your parents' grandchild, indeed their only grandchild."

"Let me get this straight, Serena, if I may—you think his parents had you knocked out by a third party so they could steal your daughter. It's the stuff of novels; far-fetched and preposterous. Forgive me if I find myself unable to jump on board with your theory. What say you Mr Barker?"

Three heads swing his way simultaneously as he takes his time, clearly enjoying being in the spotlight.

"I see all your points of view indeed I do; however, I do think it a worthy line of enquiry, especially as we have precious little else to go on. People do the strangest things for love; this I can tell you. If you think about it carefully, the Carter-Knowles's have no idea Miss Wilton-Robbins has such an influential party on her side. To them she has wronged them and has been the victim of her own, forgive me, disreputable behaviour. Perhaps they see their son as lacking in maturity to be a father. They in turn have money and influence—something they assume she is lacking. If they truly believe Hannah is their own flesh and blood then would they not, like you, do anything to rescue her from what they perceive to be a life of poverty and servitude. The question now is where would they hide her?"

Leaning my forehead into my hand, I try to think. Surely their home would be too risky.

Mr Barker's intelligent words roll around my mind as we sit in silence, only the distant sound of the ritual of clog making as background audio.

Finally, I sit up in my chair.

"I know exactly where she is," I proclaim.

The gentlemen turn as one, but I simply ask them to be good enough to accompany me on one more journey.

Oh, how I hope I am right.

However, by the time we're climbing aboard the carriages once more, my theory doesn't seem quite so preposterous any longer.

Chapter 30

I glance over my shoulder and see everyone is in position.

Dicken is to my right obscured behind a climbing rose by the door; and Dawson and Mr Barker are behind the pagoda ready to be of assistance should this be required, perish the thought.

I reach for the door handle then pull my hand away. This happens twice so Dicken takes matters into his own hands and opens the door. My heart plummets as we share a glance knowing there's no going back for us now. He swings his eyes towards the house in encouragement, so I take one last silent sigh as I step over the threshold.

A clattering from the kitchen drifts my way from down the hallway and the first voice I hear is Milner's.

"I don't know, she expects me to make a feast from a famine that one. It's like five loaves and two fishes in this house is it not, Mary?"

I hear Mary chuckle quietly thinking she must be new as I don't recognise the name. I stand by the scullery door a moment, trying to gauge if they might be leaving the room shortly. Beckoning with my hand Dicken appears, and I lead the way as we head up the steps together. At the top, the silence on the other side of the door envelopes me with an eerie sensation because I know they're at home. I'd like to catch them in the act, so I wait a moment.

How would they have explained the arrival of a small baby in the house to the gossiping staff I wonder. Discretion was never Milner's strong suit.

I'm startled by the sound of Moira's voice and grasp Dicken's hand instinctively.

"Bernard, I thought you had made all the necessary arrangements. Are you telling me now that you haven't?"

"I have dear, don't worry, everything is under control," my father says, and I lean into the sound of his voice for a second. I've missed his voice, which is about the sum of what I've missed in this house.

Even up to the point of entering I hoped I might be wrong but as I listen, my suspicions are confirmed. Hannah is here, they have my daughter, I'm somehow certain of it and my patience has run out.

I stride across the hallway and enter the study. I care not one jot about the look on their faces as they see Dicken and I appear from nowhere.

Before I even speak my eyes scour the room for signs of Hannah's presence in the house, but I find nothing, not a toy, a napkin …. nothing.

"What the …" Moira says loudly, "Where the bloody hell have you two come from?"

For once there's no sign of her fake accent, her Yorkshire dialect clear as a babbling stream.

"Never mind that, where is my daughter?" I demand.

I stand firm, full of bravado which appeared just when I needed it. Nothing and nobody will stand in my way now.

My father and Moira exchange glances. They hold each other's eyes just long enough to give the game away.

"Serena, my dear I've been very worried. I couldn't find you, I'd no clue where you went when you ran from us that day," my father says.

His painful attempt at a smile is pathetic, looking older, far older than I remember and his years. Perhaps he may truly have been worried after all.

But I have no time for niceties today. I must know the truth.

"Papa, I'm frantic about Hannah. I know we parted on bad terms, but I also know you would never want me to feel the distress I've felt these past days. Please, I beg you, tell me where my baby is."

"Oh, is that her name; why on earth would you think we have her? What on earth would we want with your fatherless spawn?" Moira says, spitting out each word for effect.

Her face is contorted with disgust, her cheeks flushed.

Dicken takes a step forward.

"Madam, I suggest you speak with more decorum," he says.

She closes her mouth and steps back.

My father shakes his head at his wife then turns to me.

"Is she here, papa?" I ask, my voice smaller but still strong. I'm appealing to his better nature.

"No, Serena, I hate to be the one to disappoint you but you're sadly mistaken, you'll not find your daughter in these four walls."

His eyes betray his lie all the while he speaks.

"I've had enough of this, Serena. Let us check the house for ourselves," Dicken says.

My father pulls him back by the arm, but Dicken shrugs him off like an irksome little fly. I rush to join Dicken in his search, but Moira grabs hold of my hair, pulling it with such force I must grab the roots to waylay the pain. Dicken now bats her hand away and knocks loudly on the window to raise the alarm with our allies.

Within what seems only seconds Dawson and Mr Barker appear looking aghast at the pandemonium in the room.

I hardly recognise my own father, scuffling with Dicken and using foul language.

"Stop this now!" I hear Dawson bellow above the sound of Moira's yelling.

Everyone stops in startled unison and turns his way.

My scalp is throbbing and I put a hand to my head amazed to find she hasn't drawn blood.

"Is Hannah here?" Dawson asks looking down at me, his voice gentler.

I nod frantically.

"I'm certain she is here but they're both denying it. We want to check the house for ourselves."

"Over my dead body," Moira pipes up.

"You know common assault amounts to a prison sentence, do you not?" Dawson tells her, "There are plenty of witnesses to testify to the fact … and I'm not only talking about what happened just now."

She lets out a guffaw at his words.

"You won't go to the police and well you know it. We wouldn't be in this situation in the first place if you weren't wanting to avoid a scandal."

"I assure you, Mrs Wilton-Robbins a scandal is the least of our worries. We only wish for a child to be returned to her rightful place, with her mother, nothing more."

Moira looks my way taking in the sight of me. I haven't eaten or slept for days so I can only imagine what she's thinking.

"She can't look after her right; she hasn't got a penny to her name. Oh, how far miss high and mighty has fallen," she sneers.

And how this woman hates me, I think though she doesn't know the first thing about me. It must have been the happiest moment of her life when I fled the house that morning.

I watch Dawson throw back his shoulders trying to hold his temper.

"Not that it's any business of yours, madam but Hannah is very well provided and cared for.

Moira stares at him but decides to hold her tongue.

I glance at my father and wonder if he was only complying with his wife's wishes. If this was the case, she didn't want Hannah so she could give her a better life, she only wanted to cause me untold misery. The jealousy this woman has towards me is out of control.

I see now my father has become a weak and malleable man. A man who would allow himself to be manipulated at the expense of the happiness and welfare even of his own daughter and granddaughter. I can barely look at him.

Dicken opens the door for me.

"Mr Barker and I will stay here while you search the house," Dawson says his eyes never leaving my father and Moira.

As I step into the hallway, I hear the door close to the scullery stairs. The staff will have been listening at the door enjoying the show. Perhaps our washing will be aired in public after all. I truly couldn't care less anymore.

Checking this floor of the house I know is pointless even as I'm running between each room. I bound up the stairs to continue and scour the seven rooms on the second floor including my old bedroom. But there's not a single sign of Hannah at all. A baby is not easy to hide. The attic houses the bedrooms of the servants, and I don't hesitate to continue with my search despite prying into their personal spaces. Flinging back door after door my panic increases each time when I fail to see my baby daughter behind it.

"She's not here, Dicken, they're telling the truth, she's not here," I tell him, my voice fraught and strange even to my own ears.

"Perhaps she's at your house. Yes, that's it, she must be there after all," I say, grasping at the last straw I can think of.

He looks unconvinced. I would much prefer not to see such signs of doubt at this moment, I think. In any case, I shall be heading to Wentworth with or without Dicken.

"It's only that I visit Wentworth often and Rowena lives there, so I can't imagine she would be hiding at mama and papa's, Serena. They've hidden her somewhere else; we must head downstairs and speak to them again," he leans against the wall, "she could be anywhere."

I set off quickly to go downstairs then stop suddenly when I hear a small voice.

"Miss, please don't distress yourself any further."

Whipping around, I see a young girl, who I assume is Mary the new maid, standing on the landing behind me.

"Come with me," she says.

She gesticulates with her head for us to follow her.

Down one flight of steps we go, then another until we finally descend the stone stairs to the scullery. Milner is waiting in the kitchen, her face taut and looking anywhere but in my direction. There will be consequences for their actions, Moira will see to that.

"Please, Miss Serena, we'd no idea the baby was yours. The mistress said she's helping her niece who has a violent husband. I hope you believe me."

"I do believe you, Milner," I say quickly without really thinking, "where will I find my daughter?"

She points to a Welsh dresser which on closer inspection I see is covering a doorway. How odd I never knew of the door's existence all the years I lived here but then I barely ventured into the kitchen. I look between the housekeeper and the doorway my body shaking. Surely not, I think, surely, they haven't kept my sweet baby locked up behind there.

"Don't worry," Mary says quickly, "It's an old storeroom. I've lit a fire and made her very comfortable in there. We go in all the time to see her, and you'll find her to be fit and well, the same as she left you."

Her words fade as Dicken leaps at the dresser, dragging it aside and I barge open the door. There on the flagged floor I see my little Hannah sitting on a threadbare rug by the fire; she has Mallers the bear at her side and her pram is in the corner of the room. Lifting herself to stand at one of two fireside chairs she beams a toothy smile in my direction.

I rush to gather her in my arms and smother her warm face with kisses. She doesn't smell like my daughter, but she soon will again I'm sure of it. I will never let her go again.

"Dada," she says, and I catch my breath.

Dicken's face lights up before he wraps us both in his strong arms. This time the word is like an angel singing in my ear.

My world is whole once more.

Chapter 31

"Well, if nothing else, the bairn hasn't been neglected that's for sure, I think they've fattened her up," Martha says.

Alicia and I grin broadly at each other, peace of mind found at last after all the turmoil.

"I doubt very much my stepmother will have given much in the way of tender loving care for Hannah, so thank goodness for Milner and Mary," I say.

"I'd hate to be in their shoes at the moment," Martha says.

"Never fear, Dawson says that if he hears of their dismissal, he wouldn't want to be in your father and stepmother's shoes," Alicia says, "I'm going for a lie down, so I'll see you both in a while."

Martha runs a finger over my cheek with a soft smile about her lips then follows her mistress from the room.

I haven't been able to put Hannah down since I found her. It will become an unhealthy obsession if I don't curb it soon.

Dicken and Dawson have decamped to Dawson's study. On the other side of the study door, I suspect they are hatching some plan for our future amongst other things. I'm not ready for making plans, not yet and I doubt for a while. For the moment I only wish to bask in the glow of my reunion with Hannah. In the dead of night there were more than a few times when I thought it might never happen.

Martha returns to the parlour and puts some coal on the fire.

"Why don't you both go up? You look all in, Little Robin. I think you'll sleep like a top tonight," she says.

"I'll wait until Dicken comes out, Martha. I think it only fair considering all he's done."

She tuts, saying, "I beg your pardon, Serena but today is a day for speaking plainly: He is her father after all, it's only right he pulls his finger out."

I laugh so loudly I startle Hannah.

"Oh, Martha, if this is what speaking plainly amounts to you can do it all the time for me."

"Well now here's a happy sound if ever there was one," Dawson says, appearing from the doorway.

I can see Dicken over his shoulder, smiling at us.

"Anybody would think there was something to celebrate."

I can't imagine I will ever stop celebrating, I think.

"Serena, would you spare me a moment of your time?" Dicken asks.

I'm not equipped for this conversation in mind or body, but I trail towards him.

"Go into my office the two of you, there's much to discuss but perhaps tomorrow will be the time for detail."

I'm grateful for the comment, Dawson can see how weary I am. Following Dicken into the study with our daughter on my hip, I close the door behind us. The silence within the room is a contrast and I think it will be the first time I've sat in here without Dawson other than to tend it. I picture him sitting behind his huge walnut desk and wish he was with us now.

Dicken and I sit opposite each other like old friends in the chairs by the fire. He smiles at me before his eyes drop to Hannah.

"Would you mind if I held her?" he asks, his voice hesitant, almost struggling to ask the question.

I don't want to let her go but I must nip the fear in the bud; and we have nothing to fear from Dicken. I pass Hannah to sit on his knee and they share their first smile as I look on.

"I think from now on you have no need to ask, Dicken. I realise she is as much a part of you as she is a part of me. So much has changed for us today. I'm ashamed now for doubting you."

"How very magnanimous of you, Serena, but I think it's only right that I should earn my daughter's affections."

He sounds so different. There's no sign of the Dicken of old, the assured arrogance has disappeared though it's still early days in our new life. As I watch him bounce Hannah slightly awkwardly on his knee I wonder if our own love could be rekindled. There's a long road ahead before then, I think, I'm getting ahead of myself.

"What happened when you spoke with Anabelle?" I ask now.

He looks across the top of our daughter's head saying, "The conversation went the way you might imagine. Divorce is out of the question she says but I hold a trump card on that front."

My eyebrows raise; what could he mean?

"If I may speak frankly, perhaps a little too candidly …" he pauses.

"Yes, as Martha says, I consider today a day for honesty," I say.

He sighs, "Well how to put it … our marriage has never been consummated," he says, his face burning, "I took advice from my solicitor, and it seems that under such circumstances the marriage may be annulled," he pauses, "I know now why I lacked interest in Anabelle. My mind and heart lay elsewhere."

My own mind reels at such a revelation. He's been thinking about me all these months after all, pining for me even by the sound of it.

"Nevertheless Dicken, marriage is marriage and I implore you, please do not pursue a divorce purely on my account. I really have no idea what will become of me, of us. I like it here and more importantly, Hannah is settled. This last week has shown me just how much she's loved by everyone at Mallerby."

I think of Mr Slater and his expression when he saw Hannah was safe, how he left the room so overcome with emotion he was unable to speak.

"Forgive me, I thought you felt the same. We share a child, and surely this is the most significant connection two people can have."

I shake my head, sighing.

"You're right of course, but what I realise now is you don't need to be connected by blood to be bonded," I smile to soften my words, "Dicken, you must understand if it wasn't for Martha Wainwright and Dawson Mallerby, I dread to think what might have become of us. It would more than likely have been the workhouse for me with Hannah whipped from my arms at the very moment of her birth."

He strokes Hannah's cheek, her face full of sleep then hangs his head.

"I will never forgive myself for my behaviour, Serena. I thought I could have it all on a platter with you and a respectable marriage. But what I didn't know then was I am in love with you. I've learned my lesson and given time I pray I can prove my love for you. Please allow me the opportunity."

Hannah has fallen asleep on his chest, her tiny head nestled into his neck so I can only see her growing mop of curls. All awkwardness toward his daughter has disappeared, so distracted was he by the sincerity of his feelings. I swallow, overcome by the sweet little scene. We are a family, a family tied and bound by blood and our daughter would have two parents who loved her by her side throughout the trials and tribulations of life.

"I think I just need time, Dicken," I say.

I simply cannot find it in me to quash his genuine affection. I'm suddenly weary almost to my bones as if I've swum an ocean.

"And time you shall have, my love," he says, the tears in his eyes pulling at my heart.

"May I just ask you one question, though I don't deserve to hear the answer, not yet?"

I nod briefly, thinking I might know the question already. I mentally begin to prepare my response as we must not start our next chapter with lies and platitudes, we must move forward with full disclosure.

"Do you love me?" he asks.

I don't answer immediately, instead I force myself to look directly at him.

"I thought I loved you once, Dicken, but now I'm not as certain as I was."

He drops his cheek to rest on the top of his little daughter's head. She's content and doesn't stir.

"Well, I must put this right for the sake of all three of us. Just know this, Serena, I know an apology alone is never enough."

"I believe you," I say and mean it.

We sit for a while in easy silence. This is what life could be like always, I think.

Eventually I get to my feet and gently remove Hannah from his arms. I sink into the comfort of her tiny body wrapping itself around me.

"Thank you for helping me," I tell him smiling gently down at him.

We walk from the room almost like a little family.

Almost.

"If I came to collect you both in my carriage, would you come to Wentworth to see my parents and Rowena?" he asks, "I know they would love to be part of Hannah's life too, and Rowena is keen to see you and her again. I intend to stay at Wentworth for the time being."

"Of course, we will be glad to," I say.

I look up at him.

"What will happen in terms of your father should all this get out. Will it be very bad for him if there is a scandal?" I ask.

Sighing, he shrugs his shoulders.

"My father is the lynchpin of the bank, and I think he has earned sufficient standing to ride out the failings of an impetuous and errant son. I hope the board will put their business interests first, but socially, now that is a very different matter.

For me at least his personal integrity is unsurpassable, and he will certainly want to do the right thing by his granddaughter," he pauses, "I know Rowena disclosed our secret, then in turn so did my father but he can't have known the consequences at the time. He doesn't know your stepmother as we do."

I touch his arm with my free hand.

"Dicken, I don't blame your mother and father for disclosing Hannah's whereabouts, I hope you won't either. They thought they were doing the right thing in being loyal to my father, and Moira will have taken great pleasure in hoodwinking them. I'm sure she will have schemed and plotted to mislead them into thinking this was a better option for Hannah's future.

I know Hannah will benefit greatly from having your family in her life. I've always admired them as you know only too well."

Smiling sadly, he pats my hand on his arm.

There's a potent atmosphere in the fabric of the household tonight as we say our farewells to Dicken. Our emotions are heightened as we're all too aware the day could have turned out so differently. We troop up the stairs, glad to draw a line under such a momentous day.

And as I climb the stairs to the attic to return my daughter safely to her rightful place, I look over my shoulder and watch Dawson Mallerby return to his own rightful place:

His marital bedroom.

Chapter 32

"Are you certain?"

Alicia nods and my heart leaps and falls like one of those terrifying fairground rides. I'm conflicted but, in the end, the right thing to do thankfully prevails.

"I'm delighted for you, for both of you," I tell her genuinely.

The other strands of my emotions will have to be clipped forever if I'm to remain part of the broader picture.

"You really mustn't say anything yet, Serena, I'm so early into the pregnancy and I must wait until the danger has passed. I couldn't bear to disappoint Dawson.

I cover her hand with my own, giving it a gentle squeeze. I'd like her to feel my empathy as I can only imagine how concerned she must be right now, her happy time shrouded in painful memories.

Mr Slater has served afternoon tea in the garden room. Spring seems far away, but the temperature is pleasant under the glass, the sunshine flooding the ferns and orchids surrounding us.

The three months since November have been relatively quiet and tranquil, one day flowing into the next with gentle ease.

We had a particularly enjoyable festive period, showering Hannah with gifts both bought and handmade. Marthas was my favourite—a clumsily handknitted red scarf—it positively glows with love every time I wrap it around her. I can picture Martha sitting by the fire in the kitchen before she retired for the evening, knitting slowly, her lips pursed in concentration. Busy yet content still at the end of a hard, working day.

On Christmas night Alicia was nodding asleep in her chair and decided it best if she went up to bed. I should have left with her, she looked over her shoulder expecting me to be there, I think, but the hour was young. I reached for my new book and stared through the pages a while.

"I confess I miss our chats, Serena," Dawson said, "I shouldn't but I do."

I touched the golden heart necklace Alicia bought for me. I opened the tiny package bound with velvet ribbon only hours before, enthralled by the delicate engraving of a bird. It was impossible to know but she was sure it was a little robin she told me. It meant more as it was chosen especially for me by my friend.

"So much has happened good and bad since those days, Dawson."

We stared at each other a moment, there was so much I would have liked to discuss with him, but it wasn't the right thing to do in our newfound situation. My eyes wandered to the tree, still alight with candles. Some had seen an end to their Christmas day.

I must go up," I said quietly, "Goodnight, Dawson and … merry Christmas."

I was shocked by his hand reaching for mine, snatching it away like it was on fire.

"Forgive me," he said, "but I don't want you to go, not yet. Will you just sit with me awhile until the fire dies."

As I looked into his eyes, I recalled the night we'd made love, those sad, green eyes breaking my heart afterwards.

"It may be some months before we get another chance. That is, if you intend staying here."

I did as he asked, and we sat in silence listening to the crackle of the fire. This time next year where will I be, I wondered.

"Good night, Serena and a merry Christmas," he said quietly as I stood to leave.

He stared at me, so my heart almost stopped, and I lowered my eyes from what he was saying to me without words. I couldn't allow myself to hear it.

*

Since the trauma of last autumn, I've visited Wentworth House weekly and more over the festive season. Dicken's mother was full of remorse when I first returned to the fold.

"I don't hold you responsible, Mrs Carter-Knowles, I know my stepmother will have been very persuasive," I told her.

"Please, after all these years I think it's about time for you call me Georgina," she nodded in the direction of Dicken's father, "and my husband, Herbert. We are to be family after all."

She'd presumed too much too soon, and I was thankful for Rowena putting in a timely appearance.

"Oh, Serena, how wonderful it is to have you back at Wentworth again. The house hasn't been the same, has it mama?"

"No, indeed it hasn't," Georgina said quietly, her affection plain for me to see.

It would be the easiest thing in the world to slip back into the family and continue my sisterly bond with Rowena. They are good, kind people, their only flaw was spoiling their son and heir.

On New Year's Day, Hannah spent the afternoon being cooed and bounced, revelling in the attention, and delighting all of us in taking a few faltering steps.

"We have a surprise for you, dear," Georgina said when Hannah settled on her knee.

"For me?"

She nodded, smiling broadly, hardly able to conceal her excitement.

"Let us just say we're hoping it might get the year off to a good start."

Dicken held my eyes as he helped me from my seat. Placing my hand in the crook of his arm he accompanied me to the library at the back of the house.

"Wait here a moment if you will," he said.

He had an odd expression as he knocked on the door and then retreated back to the dining room, glancing at me over his shoulder as he disappeared. Every nuance so far had indicated a pleasant surprise was in store.

So, when seconds later the door opened my heart plummeted with disappointment—the person waiting to see me was my father.

"Happy New Year, Serena," he said quietly.

His voice was hesitant, his smile shy, and it never occurred to me to return the greeting.

He stood to one side and after a second or two in which I considered turning on my heels, I finally entered the room. It was as though I was in a trance as I sat in the leather wing chair by the fire, my father in the chair opposite. I couldn't help myself thinking of Dawson and his library at home, a flood of homesickness making me close my eyes briefly.

When I opened them, my father's gaze was unsteady with pensiveness.

I was ambushed, wrongfooted, though I knew they only wanted us to resolve the rift between us.

"Before I start, I think you should know that your stepmother is no longer living at Walton Manor."

This pulled me from my stupor. Moira gone; out of the picture. Once this would have been my wish come true, yet I felt nothing.

"Serena, I can only apologise unreservedly for the distress we caused you."

"I see," is all I could think to say.

We sat quietly as I tried to align my wayward emotions. Until that moment I had never considered there could be reconciliation with my father.

"I must ask, did she leave, or did you ask her to leave?"

He knew the implication behind the question well enough. I watched for clues he was lying to me.

"She couldn't possibly stay after what happened. I've been weak, Serena, misguided by something, a fear of facing the future alone I think, but now I know I would never have been alone if I'd spent time with you. I've made so many mistakes and … and I miss you."

We had never spoken to each other in such a way before and a heat crept up my face.

"If you'd found out where I was living you could have spoken to me, paid a visit to Mallerby Hall. All the upset could have been avoided."

"Would you have come home, let me see my granddaughter?" he asked.

Staring out at the dormant winter grounds of Wentworth, frost had covered the lawn and the fine sculptures amongst the ivy. Dusk was already descending.

"I admit I wouldn't have come home but perhaps I may have visited with Hannah when you were alone."

His eyes were tired, and I noticed his hair had thinned over the months making him a shadow of the father I grew up with. The one I admired as every girl should and least of all because of his hair. There was much to admire about my father then.

"I couldn't allow her to be infected by that terrible woman, you only know some of what it was like for me. Life was quite intolerable when you weren't there and that was often."

"Then tell me of it, tell me all of it. I deserve to bear the burden with you, even try as your father to take it from you if I can."

Shaking my head, I told him it would serve no purpose to remember my time under my stepmother's so-called care. I was determined not hand her the power of reliving it.

"I have a question I've become fixated upon. It gives me no pleasure to ask it," I say.

I watched his face tighten as did his shoulders, his back like he was preparing for battle. Perhaps he knew already what was afoot.

"When mama was dreadfully ill those last two years, we shared many conversations before she died some more … upsetting than others. We could always be open and honest with each other, and this is what I miss the most. You know how close we were, papa, peas in a pod you used to call us."

My bottom lip began to tremble, and I couldn't look at him, but I had to go on.

"I must ask you for my own sanity: were you in a relationship with Moira before mama died?"

He jumped to his feet, startling me.

"How low I have become in your esteem that you could even entertain such a notion, Serena. I loved your mother; we were as one."

Walking to the French doors, he stared at the grounds for some time, his back to me but I could still imagine the expression on his face. When his shoulders slumped, I knew what mama and I had suspected in those dark months and years, what we feared, was the truth.

I wanted to yell, run towards him and beat his chest, tell him she deserved a husband who was loyal to the end, a husband who didn't desert her in her hour of need and worst of all, for woman such as Moira.

Instead, I rose and smoothed my hair and skirts to make my exit. There was nothing left for me to stay for.

"I would be grateful if you could make your excuses to Mr & Mrs Carter-Knowles," I said, glancing over my shoulder. He still had his back to me.

"You have grown hard, Serena," he said, "this is not an admirable quality in a woman."

As he turned from the doors, I faced him head on, though his words cut me.

"Perhaps wise may be a better choice of word, papa. In any case you need never suffer my company in the future as I'd rather our paths didn't cross again. A girl should admire her father, look up to him, rely on him, and I will never be able to do any of these things. I did once; it's so much harder to have it and lose it."

One tear hurtled down his cheek and he didn't check it. He only swallowed, his eyes lowering to the rug.

"I will go but before I do, I only ask if you will do something in memory of your mother."

My strength was failing but he knew my mother would be the one thing to stop me from walking away.

"If I find it to be appropriate to her memory," I said flatly.

He wiped his nose with his handkerchief as I waited. I mustn't weaken, I thought.

"As you know your mother was of independent means and I know that she wanted you to have this once you came of age. Even if you are unable to accept her estate for yourself, I know it would mean a great deal to her if you and eventually Hannah had your independence secured. The money is yours, Serena."

Should I throw the offer back in his face for instant gratification, I wondered. It was tempting. But by the time my hand was on the doorknob I had made my decision. I am a mother and I have my daughter to think of.

"I will accept papa but only to honour mama's memory and to give Hannah the life she deserves, a life mama would wish for her as much as I do," I said. I didn't turn around.

Then I stepped out of the room and said goodbye to my old life once and for all. I felt as though I was a phoenix, rising from the ashes, reincarnated.

But in my heart, I knew I would … I will, always remain Martha's Little Robin.

Chapter 33

"This is perfect," I say running my fingers along the black kitchen range.

The cottage is exactly what I've been looking for. Small and more than adequate for our needs; it already has a feeling of home.

I see Dicken's head turn in my direction from the corner of my eye, then follow me around as I inspect the room.

Mrs Pollard looks delighted at my assessment of the cottage. I can see she's taken great care of it and there will be little for me to do other than add my own touches.

"Are you certain Mr Pollard is agreeable to the sale of the house and adjoining land? I'd like to draw up an agreement with my solicitor immediately so my daughter and I can settle in as quickly as possible. I did say that I would prefer a sale rather than a leasehold agreement."

"Oh yes, miss, he has no use for it any longer so it may as well make somebody a good home but are you sure this is a fit home for you and your daughter? It's years since anybody's lived here, but as you can see, we've kept it in good order," she pauses wondering whether to continue, "begging your pardon, miss but it is humble accommodation for someone of your standing."

I give her a genuine smile thinking the cottage appears to have been sitting here patiently waiting for us to buy it.

"It's perfect Mrs Pollard, just perfect."

She glances between Dicken and me. I imagine she's trying to establish our connection.

"Well, I'll leave you to look around properly in our own time. Just take a walk up to the farmhouse when you're ready, my husband will be back then."

She closes the back door and I watch her walking up the track to return home. The farmhouse is well out of sight so Hannah and I will have plenty of privacy.

"So, I see you're set on buying," Dicken says now.

I look around the homely kitchen making a mental list of the furniture and paraphernalia I'll need to set up our first home.

"Serena, if I'm honest I thought you might rent somewhere for a while and give yourself time to think about our future," he says.

"I refuse to be rushed into a decision, Dicken. Please don't back me into a corner, it will be no good for either of us."

He rakes a hand through his hair then pulls a chair from under the old table.

"Could you not stay at Wentworth, just for a while? This arrangement seems so permanent."

He's pushing too hard.

"A house can always be sold," I tell him, "For now, I'd like somewhere of our own for Hannah and for me to live alone. I can't possibly decide my next step until I've created space in my mind. It must happen naturally. I hope you can understand, Dicken but if you can't, I'm afraid it will happen anyway."

It's unacceptable to remain at the hall now Alicia is pregnant, and the situation is becoming quite insufferable. It has made me feel like an outsider, an imposter even. Dawson is still in the dark about the baby, though I think she might tell him soon. So, my plan is to be installed in here as soon as possible.

I pull out the other chair to join Dicken at the table. The sun is streaming in from the window highlighting the patina of the wood. This table is dappled with all the memories of a life, lives even. I can see it clearly and how perfect it will be to add our story to it.

"What will you do for staff?" Dicken asks.

"I don't need staff, Dicken and there isn't really any room though I might get someone to come in and help out a few times a week. I wouldn't have thought it once, but I know I'll be happy building a little nest in this cottage, caring for Hannah here. I'm in easy walking distance of the hall so everyone can still see plenty of her."

He sighs realising he's beaten, at least for the time being.

"Alright then if you must make me wait, if that's what you really want then I'll wait," he says sullenly.

That spoiled little boy is back, only confirming I'm making the right decision. I need time.

"Mama and papa will be disappointed, as will Rowena. I think they've been thinking along the same lines as I have."

"Dicken," I say with a tinge of my own exasperation, "you forget you are still a married man. You have plenty to be getting on with for the foreseeable future. If you still wish to pursue a divorce, an annulment even you must get the ball rolling. Then you must take some time to let the dust settle, it wouldn't be proper to marry you immediately, even if I wanted to."

He grasps both my hands in his across the table.

"That's what I want Serena, I've told you many times you are my love, my future yet it appears you think me trite and insincere still."

I touch his cheek and smile attempting to smooth his feathers.

"I know you truly believe the words, but we haven't had a taste of real life yet. We haven't had to deal with disappointment, boredom and all the other harsh realities. Reality is far different to dreams surely you know this after your brief marriage."

I think of Dawson and Alicia and the turmoil they both faced for years. Real life is often challenging in one way or another and not for the faint hearted. Dicken still has so much growing up to do.

"You know Mrs Pollard is right; you'll be quite the oddity around these parts. A woman of your standing and income living as a single parent in a tiny cottage, coming and going to the village shop in your fine gowns."

I laugh so hard I spill a tear, taking huge clumps of air to prevent myself becoming hysterical. He's quite right of course, but then Dawson has taught me one very important lesson:

Happiness is far more important than convention. My reputation may be sullied for evermore no matter how respectable I become.

I continue to think of Dawson. I can almost hear his thoughts on the subject now as I sit in what I already consider my new kitchen.

"The villagers would do well to mind their own damn business!" he would say, though his choice of words would be stronger if he weren't talking to a lady.

I couldn't agree more.

Chapter 34

"They've been at it for an hour now," Martha tells me as I hang up my coat, "Disappointingly the commotion is loud enough to notice from the scullery, but not so loud I can hear what's going on."

Chuckling, I stop when I hear a door slamming then a small sob. I stand still on the other side of the stairs until I hear yet another door slam. Martha and I gawp at each other like fish in a bowl then scurry when we hear Dawson's heavy tread on the stairs going above our heads. As I'm fleeing, I'm thinking this Sunday afternoon has taken an unexpected turn.

"I'd wait a minute or two, Mr Slater if I was you before you take that tray up.

He places the tray back on the table, dropping his arms and looking as though he has no idea what to do with himself now his routine has been interrupted.

"Let's have a brew ourselves and then I'll do a fresh pot in five minutes," Martha says.

I'm always thankful for her pragmatic approach, I think as I swing Hannah into my arms and play peekaboo with my free hand. Mr Slater joins in. Playing with Hannah is the one time he looks at ease. He's a natural with children but I never point this out in case I make him self-conscious. I would hate to spoil the magic.

"Serena, I would be grateful if you could join me a moment in the drawing room. Slater, please bring the tea tray up too if you will."

My head swings around to see Dawson standing at the bottom of the scullery stairs. He's never ventured below stairs before to my knowledge, I think as I jump from my seat and hand Hannah to Martha. As I head upstairs behind him, I feel something is horribly wrong.

Once in the drawing room Mr Slater glances at me as he sets down the tea tray and I give him a tight smile. The atmosphere is very sombre, and I busy myself pouring tea as a distraction.

"I'm sorry to summon you in such a way, Serena, but I must speak with you urgently."

I hand him a cup, and he holds up his palm. My heart is throbbing in my mouth wondering what I might have done. I sit in silence thinking he can't be angry about the cottage surely because I mentioned it. I didn't want to be underhand.

"I'm not upset with you," he says, "So you needn't sit there looking like a child waiting to be scolded."

Raising his eyes to heaven he sighs then clams his mouth shut. I take a sip of tea and wait for him to settle himself.

"I think I must start at the beginning if you're to understand what it is I'm about to disclose to you. What you see is not what it appears and I fear you may have been misled," he says, cryptically.

I shuffle in my chair, uncomfortable for so many reasons.

"Dawson, please just get on with what it is you must say to me."

His eyes widen at my tone.

"Alright then, I will. So, it is no secret that my wife and I have always had a tempestuous relationship. I know Martha and Slater are the height of discretion and I value this in my staff above all else. However, I think perhaps you misread my feelings about my wife's prolonged absence. I think you may have thought I was missing her and desirous of her return when you went on your little adventure to find her and bring her home. Am I correct?"

I nod but don't speak.

"Alicia is a kind woman and a difficult woman in equal measure, her mother may have told you this. She seeks attention but the more she sought this from me the less I wanted to give it. She tried many schemes to keep me from my work and by her side, but this became a strangle-hold leaving me struggling to breathe.

Yes, I was unhappy my marriage had failed. I also felt responsible for the lengths she went to improve our relationship. But these were as nothing in comparison to her behaviour toward me."

He stops talking now whilst my mind tries to work out exactly what the lengths Alicia went to were.

"I can only try and explain the situation in simple terms. Three times my wife informed me she was pregnant … and three times they ended in miscarriage, or so she told me. This was obviously distressing but can you imagine how I felt when I eventually found out these were all lies."

My jaw slackens and I let out a small gasp.

Surely not, I think, I find it unthinkable my good friend, his wife would stoop to such a level.

"How do you know she told lies, Dawson?" I ask.

He reaches for his teacup then gulps the entire contents, clinking it back onto the saucer on the tray.

"I know because after the first time I asked the doctor what I could do to help her, perhaps a visit to a specialist in Harley Street. Dr Cheadle had no knowledge of a pregnancy. I didn't speak of it further each time wanting to believe she might be telling the truth. But on the third occasion the doctor said that he must intervene for all our sakes. He had wanted to prescribe some medication to settle her nerves but foolishly I refused and then events took an unexpected turn when she left with Larry."

He stops speaking a moment and hangs his head.

"So there never were any pregnancies, Serena."

It's too much; it's too much to think of Dawson being handed such false hope. To be told he was to become a father and then the dream being snatched cruelly away not once, not twice but three times. And all to gain his attention.

"After finding out about her affair, I asked her to live at her mother's though she had no idea I knew about the false pregnancies."

His face is sallow, haunted and I want to help take away the pain.

"Oh, Dawson, I'm so sorry," I say.

The words sound dreadfully inadequate.

He clasps both hands at the back of his neck closing his eyes.

"I know you are and I'm so unhappy, Serena, you have no idea. I know you thought you were doing the right thing in bringing my wife home and part of me really wanted that dream to come true. I even convinced myself for the sanctity of my marriage I must try once more and I have tried, believe me but it's no good, it was always a dream and now I must ask her to leave."

"Leave!" I say aghast.

"Yes, but for good this time. I will support her properly of course until such time our separation can be formalised. I wanted to tell you as we both owe you so much in trying your best to help us rebuild our love."

I think of Alicia crying in her room, alone and bereft. I should be angry with her, and I am, but this is laced with sadness.

"I'm grateful to you for telling me, but I must go upstairs and see Alicia. I must talk to her as one friend to another. I know she's done wrong by you, but sometimes desperate people do desperate things."

"I agree, she was desperate. But she was never meant to be my wife as I was never meant to be her husband. We're unable to make each other happy though we've certainly tried. I'm convinced of this now and I have you to thank for settling my mind on this."

He stares at me a moment then turns his face to the fire.

I go over to him and lay a hand on his forearm. He grips it with some force for a moment but still, he doesn't look at me.

It's a while before I can bear to walk away from my love and his obvious pain.

Then as I climb the stairs to talk with his wife, a cold shame creeps over me at the realisation I have played a central role in the ending of two marriages. Does this make me a bad person?

Whether it does or not I know it seems I must face the next chapter of my life alone for the sake of my daughter … and my own sanity.

Chapter 35

I'm all set to batten down the hatches for the evening. I look around the kitchen and bask in the cosiness of my new home and all my new things; I shall never take them for granted.

I make my way into the parlour and watch the flames of the fire rise as I broddle it with the poker. I close the curtains on the world and think how satisfying it is to have peace for both of us after so long.

Hannah's toys are tidied away into the cupboard under the stairs and my book is ready and waiting on the side table. I place the kettle on the kitchen range and turn as I hear the click of the latch on the back door.

Martha appears, knitting bag in hand and I greet her with my usual embrace as she takes her coat off to settle down for a rest. This is our nightly routine and I look forward to it.

"Tea shan't be long, Martha," I tell her, filling the teapot and setting the tray.

I don't think my family and friends will ever understand how much joy I get from the simple pleasures of life, from living simply. I sit awhile to chew the fat as she calls it with my dear friend.

Martha puts her feet up on the footstool, one of my recent acquisitions. I've thoroughly enjoyed feathering my nest.

"I'll be glad for a sit down, Little Robin, I can't lie. It's been a heck of a day at the hall, and I'm fair shattered.

"Is that the last of it then?" I ask.

I'm referring to the furniture Alicia has taken to furnish her new house on the outskirts of Leeds. She wants to be near civilisation and other people.

"Yes, the maid has moved in tonight and she wants us to visit before too long," she sighs, "I expect she'll feel cast adrift for a while."

I think she's felt that way for a very long time even within a marriage, and a so-called love affair. So much for love when Larry never even came to find her. She had a lucky escape from that man. I shiver at the memory of my one encounter with him.

"Dawson wants me to go, doesn't he?" Alicia asked, when I went to see her that Sunday in her bedroom. She was lying on her side on the four-poster bed, her nose glowing red with crying.

I perched beside her and saw the merest shred of hope in her eyes. I couldn't hold her gaze.

"What is it?" she asked.

I stroked her hand which was clutching a handkerchief.

"Alicia, this is a difficult question to ask but I must."

She propped herself up on her elbow.

"Are you still to have a baby?" I asked.

Her lower lip quivering she then pushed her face into the coverlet, so her sobs were muffled. Eventually she sat up and wiped her eyes.

"I think perhaps I may have been mistaken," she said.

"Perhaps," I said, levelly.

It wouldn't have been right to express any disapproval at this point and add to her obvious distress. What good would it have done to challenge her when she was already broken?

"Dawson would never leave me if I had a baby, he couldn't possibly. He's a decent man, an honourable one," she looked at me, "but then I think I may be preaching to the converted."

I smiled and laid my head on the many pillows, thinking of my chats on the bed with Rowena. It seemed another life ago.

"I'm sorry my plan didn't work. I was naive enough to believe love conquers all. I've since learnt my lesson believe me," I said after a while.

"Love does conquer all, Serena, I think but Dawson and I weren't ever in love, not really. I only wanted stability, status, perhaps even freedom from the ties of my mother. I never really stopped to think about love, not then. I've been losing my mind trying to cling to a man who was pushing me away. In the end I lost faith, and I regret the choice I made. That too wasn't for love though I thought it was at the time," her face crumpled, "I should have been strong like you, carved my own path instead of losing my self-respect. You had the best of intentions when you came in search of me to bring me home. I'm now free from a terrible situation with Larry and a terrible situation with Dawson—I will forever be indebted to you."

I sat up and swung my legs off the bed.

"I'll make you a strong cup of tea and then it might help if you go down and talk with Dawson calmly. Perhaps it might help you both. Though, I'm hardly an authority on relationships you understand."

We laughed, then she looked at me thoughtfully.

"Will you marry Dicken?" she asked.

She headed to the dressing table and redid her hair, powdering her nose to try and disguise the redness.

I was set to leave so her question threw me. I looked at her reflection in the mirror.

"No, I'm afraid Dicken and I aren't meant to be," I said, "I can't live in a loveless marriage, the easiest option or not. Hannah would not thrive in such a relationship any more than I would myself."

She placed her hairbrush back on the dressing table.

"Perhaps your heart belongs to another," she said lightly.

She held my gaze too long in the mirror, making me uncomfortable but then her smile shone so brightly.

So brightly in fact it upset me.

Chapter 36

"What the blazes do you think you're doing?"

I watch as Martha squares up to a man too drunk to care what he says or what he does.

Rushing to position myself between them both she only skirts around me to tuck me behind her.

I gasp as Dicken pushes Martha with such force she stumbles, losing her footing so I hear a sickening thud as she falls against the fender.

"Martha! Martha!" I shout, grabbing a towel from the rail then pressing it to her head, "Martha!"

Her eyes roll open and I shudder, the relief palpable.

"I'm alright don't fret now," she says.

"This is your fault, you're to blame for this," Dicken says too loudly, "you've been leading me on, sending me stark, staring mad. What's a man supposed to do, I ask you?"

I shrug his hand from my shoulder and swing around to face him.

"Get out!" I spit.

Stumbling backwards his lip curls and I'm fighting a terrible urge to strike him. I've never wanted to strike another human being before, not even Moira.

"You would do well to listen to the lady if you know what's good for you."

I hear Dawson's voice and see him filling the doorway over Dicken's shoulder. Comfort sweeps over me like a warm blanket.

"You!" Dicken yells, spinning around too quickly so he staggers, "You're to blame for all this. You never wanted her or *my* daughter to leave, keeping them hostage in your gilded prison."

"I'll not speak to you in this state, man. Get yourself in your carriage and be on your way home. You're not wanted here," Dawson says quietly.

"I will not be leaving without my family. I've had enough of being left hanging like some half-wit, I'll not wait any longer."

As Dicken swings his fist, Dawson steps away then grabs him by his jacket. I see Dawson's face glowering and his fist clenching, but after a second or two he thinks better of it. Instead, he drags him out of the back door.

"Stay with Martha while I send for the doctor, Serena," Dawson calls from the outside step.

With her head on my lap, Martha rests her hand on my arm. Even in such a state she's trying to placate me. Dawson, please hurry, I think.

I stare down at Martha pleading, "Martha, oh Martha don't leave me, please don't leave me."

She opens her eyes.

"Just let me sit down for a moment. I'm fine," she whispers.

Dropping my head back I send silent thanks to a higher power before I help her to the settee.

"You don't think that poor excuse of a man would get the better of me, do you? I've seen bigger men than him off."

If I could muster a smile at this moment I certainly would.

Dawson appears and pats Martha's arm, clearly relieved to see her sitting up and alert.

"Martha Wainwright, shame on you. You'll do anything for a day off," he says.

Her chuckle is like a heavenly choir.

*

"I need to wake her every hour, but I think I'll make it half-hourly to be on the safe side," I tell Dawson as I join him.

Martha needed three stitches and I got her into my bed after much protestation.

Dawson looks like he's bursting out of my small room, like he's sitting in a doll's house.

"I'll stay with you. I'm not risking Carter-Knowles coming back though I saw his carriage scarpering into the distance, fleeing like some bat out of hell," he says.

I pour him a brandy and me a sherry and settle myself on the other end of the settee.

"You appeared as if from nowhere. Why were you here?" I ask.

Swirling his glass then taking a large swig, he tells me, "Slater saw him almost fall from his carriage then stagger up the path as he was drawing the curtains. He was worried and raised the alarm to be on the safe side. I'm very glad now he did."

Dear Mr Slater, I think he's been a quiet mainstay, almost a protector to Hannah and me.

Through the night I check on Martha and begin to relax, the sherry working its magic in settling my stomach. The room is tranquil after the fracas.

"I've missed this, Serena," Dawson says.

Smiling at him, I settle back on the settee. I've been thinking the very same thought.

"I take it he's finally out of the equation," he says.

Pulling my hair loose, I run my fingers through it.

"I've come to realise he was never in the equation. He was very persuasive, convinced he was in love with me and for a time he had me convinced too."

He stares at me a moment.

"I know how he feels," he whispers so quietly I can barely hear the words.

I shake my head and stare back at him.

"Dawson, you don't love me, you love Hannah. The two are very different things."

I turn the conversation back to Dicken.

"He thought everything would return to normal once Hannah was safe but my insistence on waiting never sat easily with him. Oh, he tried, but I really always knew I didn't love him and perhaps this became evident because day by day I could see little signs of the petulant, boorish Dicken returning."

Turning to me, Dawson reaches out to touch my cheek faraway eyes telling me he hasn't been listening to a word I've been saying. I sit wide-eyed and silenced by disbelief. How can this be happening, I can't take it in.

"You think I only love your daughter?" he shakes his head and smiles, "How wrong you are, Serena, how incredibly wrong you are."

His eyes roam my face, my hair as though seeing me for the first time.

"My beautiful girl, I've loved you since the day you landed on my doorstep as Renee Robson, terrified you'd be turned out on the streets, thrown in the workhouse like some chattel. I wanted to bundle you into my arms that day and wipe away the anxiety from that frightened face. This face should only ever glow with happiness. You've suffered too much."

It slowly begins to dawn on me what he's saying. He's declaring his love for me, not just for my daughter. He loves me too. How could I have been so blinkered?

His eyes never leave mine as he watches his words sink in.

"Oh, Dawson, I genuinely thought you loved your wife, that you were longing for her to return home. That's why I searched far and wide to bring her back to you, so I didn't have to witness the sadness which hung over you like noose. It was terrible to see, to feel."

He strokes my hair from my face.

"My sadness was because I couldn't have you. I couldn't confess my love because I was married with no hope of a divorce. My love, you of all people deserve so much better than that."

His lips fall to mine in a kiss which starts tenderly then ignites to a burning fever. I thought the love I had for him, that had long been buried deep in my soul was unrequited, that his love was only for a child, the child he couldn't have yet longed for so much.

"I did it because I loved you and your happiness was everything to me," I say between each kiss.

I need this man so badly. He loves me, I feel it, I've always felt it with each glance, each touch.

Our kiss never breaks as I take control, lifting my skirts to straddle him. He gasps with surprise and moans his pleasure.

"If you want to wait, I will wait for as long as you need," he whispers.

"I don't want to wait a moment longer, Dawson, I've waited long enough.

His hands are on my thighs, pulling my underwear down, his hands now rising to my buttocks. He lifts me onto him, so I stifle a groan at the sensation it gives me.

"How I want you, how I love you," he says, burying his face into my neck as I rise and fall, gathering momentum.

"Remember Dawson, I am not only yours for tonight but for always. You have spoiled me for anyone else," I tell him as I reach the heights of my passion.

I feel him shuddering against my body as we cling to each other to savour the pleasure it brings us together.

We sit the whole night long side by side, holding hands and basking in the afterglow.

Few words are spoken; we are happy just to be in each other's company. How long we have waited for this night.

By dawn I'm certain Martha can be left alone to sleep. Dawson and I doze in each other's arms a while until Hannah wakes.

I bring her downstairs to sit between us, and I look on at my love and my daughter and wonder how life can change so quickly.

I make tea and toast some bread on the flames of the fire. I wish I could stay like this forever in this room, I think.

"Well, I suppose it's time I should be going about my business," Dawson says eventually.

I smile. "I think that's been taken care of sir," I tease.

He smiles in return. "You know, I think it only fitting I make an honest woman of you," he says, reaching to play with my unruly curls. "I don't want to start our life together with any clouds or concerns."

He drops his hand and I watch as he bobs down onto one knee.

"Therefore, Miss Serena Wilton-Robbins, will you do me the greatest honour of my life in agreeing to marry me?"

Chapter 37

"Happy the bride the sun shines on!" Martha exclaims.

I rub my eyes and stretch giving her a sleepy smile. Today is the day I become Mrs Serena Mallerby I think, excitement taking hold.

Flinging the curtains wider she says, "Come my beautiful Little Robin, let us lay the ghosts of the past to rest and have a day to treasure."

Sitting up in bed I stretch my arms out wide and she leans to give me the warmest embrace.

"Oh, Martha, I'm so happy we are sharing this day."

I touch the face I know so well. How I miss waking up to it.

"I'm not going to say what you mean to me Martha because it will make me cry, but I hope you can feel it."

"I feel it, I feel it," she says, shooing me away, "be off with you to your bath before I make a show of myself."

I stare in the mirror suddenly subdued.

"Oh, mama, how I wish you were here with me today," I whisper.

I splash my face with cold water to stem my tears.

A year has passed since Dawson's proposal. We did not announce our engagement until the legalities of separation from Alicia had been concluded and he's now free to marry albeit not in church. It's a small price to pay. Alicia admitted abandonment rather than adultery to spare her reputation and all went smoothly with the divorce as both parties were agreeable.

"It upsets me I'm unable to give you the big wedding you deserve, Serena," Dawson said one night.

I drew a line down his face, and he leaned into my hand.

"I wouldn't want a big wedding even if I could have it. I will wear the dress of my dreams though and Martha will give me away; Hannah will be a flower girl and Rowena and Alicia witnesses along with a few meaningful guests. Regardless of pomp and ceremony, it will still be the happiest day of my life, my love."

I meant every word.

News has arrived that Alicia is set to marry in the autumn to a widowed Colonel who was a friend of her father's. His no-nonsense, sensible character suits her and he's a calming influence. I wonder whether she is in love, but as she said, that was never her priority in a marriage and so I'm happy for her.

By midday I'm dressed in my gown twirling in front of my bedroom mirror. It only took an hour of searching the best establishments in Harrogate to find my dress of silk and lace. It spoke to me. It whispers around my body as my veil swirls around my shoulders.

"You make the perfect bride," Alicia says.

I smile shyly and wonder what her wedding dress was like on the day she married Dawson. I put the thought to one side and instead we share a champagne toast with Martha and Rowena.

"To friendship," Rowena says as we clink glasses repeating the sentiment.

Hannah is wearing her flower girl dress, and we stand side by side a moment smiling at each other's reflection. Swinging her into my arms I stroke her soft cheek and share a moment for mother and daughter.

They're so important to me and I make sure we share them as much possible in small ways. The love of a mother is the love that shapes you.

"By eck, you're going to be like bookends when she's older," Martha says laughing, "we'll not tell you apart."

"You all look beautiful," I tell my friends who are simply glowing in their summer dresses, all different styles but in the same colour of lavender blue. My eyes clash with Martha's and I look away quickly, tears sparkling our eyes.

Finally, the time has come to set off in my coach decorated with blue ribbon and white roses to meet Dawson, the scent of the flowers greeting me as I'm helped into the carriage. Hannah sits on Martha's knee gripping her posy tightly in her tiny hands.

I think of her father.

"I'm happy for you, Serena, really I am," Dicken said when I told him I was to marry.

He eventually returned to Anabelle who now knows about Hannah and has accepted the situation, he told me. I'm wary. There will be no repeat of the situation I was in with Moira but when they announce they are to have a baby of their own I shall feel more relaxed.

Dicken is a weak man who cannot be alone, just like my father, and it will be up to Hannah to decide if she wants to continue to have him in her life when she's older, just as I made my decision.

Dicken says he hasn't touched a drop of the demon drink since that bitter-sweet night, but I always make sure we meet at his parent's house. I'm not a fool.

My wedding is a small and intimate affair at the registry office in Harrogate and I'm grateful to be spared a day shared with dozens of distant relations and friends of my parents.

Adjusting my veil Martha tells me a story without words then stands back to admire her work.

"You'll do," she says, and we share a smile.

I heave a final breath as I hold fast to her hand and Hannah's and set off down the aisle of the registry office. I smile down at my daughter with her posy in her other hand. I'm certain I couldn't be more delighted to raise my head and return the smile of our guests if I was walking down the aisle of Westminster Abbey.

Georgina and Herbert Carter-Knowles beam my way and I see Mr Slater in his church suit dabbing an eye with his handkerchief. There's Eric and Mavis from my adventures in Halifax and they wave at us cheerfully. Mavis is clearly wearing a new hat and dress bought especially for our day. I never forgot my promise to return and see them and both. Alicia and I made an emotional trip back to the farm to see them once our lives had settled. They scarcely understand the important part they played in getting me here today, but I will never forget their kindness to a stranger in her hour of need.

Alicia's husband, resplendent in dress uniform, shares a smile with Alicia who is walking behind us with Rowena. We walk slowly and calmly as I'm determined to savour every second of the day.

Finally, and saving the best until last, I allow my eyes to look straight ahead to meet Dawson's as he waits patiently for me. Oh, how patient he has been I think and oh, how handsome he looks in his morning suit, hat under his arm and thoughtfully wearing the paisley tie I bought him as a gift.

He touches my hand gently as I arrive by his side and bends to kiss Hannah. She slides her tiny arms around his neck to the exclamation of our small congregation.

As we say our vows, we hold each other's eyes. I've waited so long and now I know I'm in my rightful place: Right by the side of Dawson Mallerby and how could I ever want to be anywhere else.

Our lips touch gently cementing our promise and he bends to lift Hannah into his arms. My throat catches with pride at my new family. Some things are worth the wait, I think.

As we turn to face our guests, Martha rushes forward to give me a hug. I plant a kiss on her wet cheek, her hat slipping to one side, so she must grab it quickly.

Outside, we're showered with confetti as Dawson helps me aboard our bridal carriage. He joins me and we share a stolen kiss. This time we linger.

"Well, there's no fleeing to be done now, Mrs Mallerby," he says, "I think you've done enough running away for one lifetime."

Laughing I push him gently with my shoulder.

"I have no need to run any longer," I say, staring into those green eyes.

How they intoxicate me.

We arrive at the Black Swan hotel and adjourn to a private room for our wedding breakfast.

"Dawson, this room is fit for royalty, it's exquisite," I say, as we walk in.

He smiles and kisses my hand. He leads me to an enormous round table in the centre of the room filled with foliage and candles. The setting is elegant but convivial, perfect for an intimate gathering.

"To Hannah Marie the First ... and of course the Second," Dawson says as he finishes his speech.

We raise a glass to the special ladies in our lives as I wipe a tear and I kiss my daughter sitting by my side now on Martha's lap. Such a beautiful sentiment, my heart is set to burst with love.

"I won't ask if this has been the day you wished for because it's written all over your face," Dawson whispers as we slope away when nobody is looking. We find a bench seat by a fountain in the nearby Valley Gardens and sit side by side. The summer night is warm, the floral splendour for which Harrogate is renowned, at its peak.

"I couldn't be happier," I say leaning my head on his shoulder, "I'm looking forward to returning to the bridal suite with my new husband."

"You are shameless, Serena Mallerby ... but I'm so glad," he chuckles.

Oh, but I'm not lying, Mr Mallerby I think, the wedding night is beckoning, enticing me. We sit a moment, the scent of jasmine strong in the heat.

When we return inside it's clear our big day is winding down. Our guests look tired or tipsy or both, ruddy-faced and ready for sleep.

"We'll be on our way up," Martha says.

"Good night, my sweetheart," I say, kissing Hannah's cheek and then Martha's, "Thank you for today, I couldn't have done it without you."

"Ay, well, I don't think you'll be needing my help from here on in," she says.

I throw my head back with laughter.

"Oh, Martha Wainwright, please don't ever change," I say as she smiles and heads towards the open staircase.

I stand watching them until they disappear then head off to find Rowena and Alicia.

They're sitting together, bouquets on the table. We eat some wedding cake and chat awhile until Rowena says she must retire.

"Goodnight, Serena, sweet dreams," she says heading off with her shoes in her hand and a twinkle in her eye, "don't forget, lunch at Wentworth when you're back from honeymoon."

"Sounds perfect," I say, throwing her a kiss and a wave.

Alone at the table now my attention turns to Alicia who is rebuttoning her shoes.

"Would you care for a little stroll, Alicia?"

She stands up and I think how beautiful she looks in her bridesmaid dress, a circlet of cream roses sitting like a crown.

"Of course, that would be very pleasant," she says.

I kiss Dawson lightly, telling him I shan't be long. His lazy smile makes me tingle as he turns from Herbert and their brandy night caps.

Alicia and I head back into the gardens, and I smile as she suggests sitting on the bench Dawson and I shared earlier. Smoothing our dresses, we sit side by side in silence for a moment in the warm breeze watching mayflies come and go from the pond lilies. The night much like the day couldn't be more evocative.

"It really has been a wonderful day, Serena, you must be walking on air."

"I am but I will feel even happier to know that you're reconciled and happy with our new lives. I know it can't have been easy for you today. To be honest, I was surprised when you accepted the invitation."

Playing with the velvet belt of her dress, she runs it between her fingers.

"I wouldn't have missed it for the world. Bernard is very fond of you both too."

"He seems a very kind man and he looked very handsome in his uniform today."

She laughs.

"I thought so too, when I saw him, my heart went all aflutter. I know he's quite a bit older, but I think he's very distinguished looking."

"For what it's worth, I think you will have a very simple and happy life together," I say, "For me a simple life equates to a peaceful one."

We turn our heads and smile at each other, then instinctively share an embrace. I sense she knows as well as I do the time has come to go back inside.

"I wish you only happiness, Serena, and Dawson too. You're clearly a match made in heaven."

My hold tightens around her slightly.

"I forgive you, Alicia," I whisper in her ear.

Pulling away sharply her eyes dart quickly between my own, staring at each other in the half-light of the summer evening.

"I'm sorry. What a very peculiar thing to say, Serena, are you quite yourself?" she asks, her voice high-pitched accompanying a small laugh.

"Perfectly," I say.

My gaze remains steady while hers can only flutter.

She submits, getting up to leave.

"I'd be grateful for just one more moment of your time," I say quietly, but with an intent that forces her to turn back and then resume her place on the bench.

"Thank you," I say, "this won't take long but it must be said. You know Alicia, it always troubled me how Moira would have known where Hannah and I were that night."

I look at Alicia's beautiful face in profile. A face which is now becoming a mask of horror.

"Once it became clear that Dicken and Rowena were not involved, I realised there had to be a go-between at the hall who had helped with the plan. The timing was too precise, to have been sheer coincidence."

She finally turns to look at me.

"I sincerely hope you're not inferring I was that person. Serena. I have only gratitude for all you have done for me, so why would I do such a thing?" she pauses, "What an absolutely appalling accusation!" she finishes too loudly.

Her face lowers to look at the grass at our feet.

"The lady doth protest too much methinks," I say theatrically, "what I find more upsetting is that for long enough I suspected Mr Slater. But as awkward as he may appear he has nothing but goodness in him and I'm ashamed to have harboured that thought for even a second."

I hear a small sob in the quietness.

"I know you weren't of sound mind when you did it, Alicia. I saw the state of you that day when I waylaid you if you recall. You have found life difficult for a long time and I imagine this is what happens when you marry the wrong person. I only want you to admit it," I say placing a hand lightly on her forearm.

I deliberately make no mention of the lies she told Dawson. That situation is between them and has nothing to do with me.

She grips my hand tightly.

"I'm so sorry, Serena, truly I am. I would never have wanted the situation to progress in the way it did," she says between sobs, "it's true, I wasn't myself and it was becoming clear that Dawson was in love with you even though you were too naïve to see it. He may have returned briefly to our marital bedroom, but I always knew I wasn't the one he wanted. I think he felt like he was being unfaithful to you when he was with me, ironic as this may sound."

Her hand goes to her mouth. How could she possibly have been pregnant if she and Dawson had never made love? She has caught herself in her own lie.

But I choose to ignore the remark as I have no wish to relive that time any further.

"I was desperate and decided to go to your house to disclose your whereabouts. Moira was home and it was soon apparent she was filled with resentment towards you, and …. oh, Serena I'm so ashamed about what happened with Hannah, the whole situation got out of hand. I didn't know what and whom I was dealing with when I met Moira."

"I know you're sorry," I say, "That's why I've decided to forgive you. I can't carry the poison of hating you around with me, it will do me no good."

Her grip tightens on my hand.

"I know you shan't want to see me again after tonight. I'll leave first thing in the morning before breakfast. I'll tell Bernard I'm feeling unwell. We can send our apologies via the front desk."

I drop my hand, getting to my feet.

"Well, I think it might be for the best."

She looks up at me with a pitiful expression.

"So much has changed since that day," she says, wiping her eyes with a curled forefinger, "I really did grow to love you and Hannah, though I wished I could have made my husband love me. I've no right to ask it, but I'd rather Dawson didn't find out."

Sighing I drop my shoulders.

"I can't begin my married life on a lie, Alicia. I shan't rush to tell Dawson but when he asks why we don't see you, I must tell him. I will however ask him not to interfere as we have dealt with the situation ourselves tonight, woman to woman."

Humiliation clouds her face as she lowers it.

"I think it might be best if I persuade Bernard we should move away."

My silence signals my view.

"For my part I will always care for you Alicia, but I don't believe I could ever trust you again. This means the foundation of our friendship is lost. I know you understand."

I turn to walk away certain I appear far stronger than I feel. This had to be done tonight, I had to hear her confession from her own lips to be able to move forward.

As I disappear into the hotel, I can feel her eyes still upon me.

It's funny how we married the same man, I think.

Yet our experience of him could not be more different.

*

"What kept you woman?" my husband asks.

He's teasing me, pulling me into his arms. Nothing bad can happen when I'm in these arms, I think.

"I'm all yours," I say.

I lean into his side as we climb the two flights of stairs to the bridal suite.

Swinging back the door I see the room is dressed to the nines with every imaginable wedding decadence. I spot a silver ice bucket chilling the finest champagne.

Dawson stoops to lift me into his arms. He sweeps me off my feet to carry me over the threshold and I squeal with shock and delight as he plonks me on the bed, laughing loudly.

This is it I think, the start of our new life is this very moment.

His tie is loose, his hair ruffled enticingly as I watch him open the champagne then pour it into our glasses.

"To my beautiful bride," he says, touching my glass with his own.

Holding his eyes, I smile then take a sip.

"Before I do his lordship's bidding," I say, "I have something I must tell you."

Kicking off his shoes, I follow suit and we lounge on the bed, face to face.

"What is it that's so important to delay the festivities?" he asks.

I trace his lips with my finger.

"Well, you know you've never been a man who is too preoccupied with convention?"

He nods, raising an eyebrow. Oh, I must find some self-control.

"Well, I'm certain this isn't the usual conversation a bride should be having with her husband on her wedding night but …"

"Get on with it, Serena, spit it out for heaven's sake you're starting to concern me."

"As you wish," I say, "so, Mr Dawson Mallerby I hereby inform you that you are to become a father …just in time for Christmas."

His eyes widen and a slow smile lifts his mouth.

"Truly?" he asks almost coyly.

I grin.

"Truly."

"Oh, Serena."

He rolls onto his back, and I lie at his side. His hand seeks mine and curls around it and we lay like this a moment.

"This is indeed the most wonderful news, on the most wonderful day, my love," he whispers eventually then turns his head, "however I think you're forgetting one important thing."

Searching his face for clues he is giving nothing away.

"And what might that be?" I ask, my stomach tightening. My nerves are far too delicate for any revelations.

"You forget I have been a father for some time. I think that honour was given to me the night Hannah Marie was born."

I can't speak for a moment.

"Oh, Dawson, how blessed we are to have you, my love," I say, tears stinging my eyes.

Now and perhaps for the very first time, I know all is well and we will be safe from harm in the future.

There was just one last item of unfinished business on my mind. Unbeknown to Dawson, I took the liberty of re-engaging the investigative skills of Mr Barker, and tomorrow morning the police will pay a call to Brook Hill, the rather rundown boarding house in Keighley my stepmother now calls her home.

If my stepmother thinks I am prepared to spend the rest of my life looking over my shoulder, she is sadly mistaken. Her cruelty to me was one thing, but kidnapping my daughter, well, a mother's love knows no bounds and the woman must be served her just desserts.

And if she decides to bring Alicia and my father down with her, then I'm afraid this is a police matter, and out of my hands. I will have to live with that; I am prepared to live with that as a sacrifice for the greater good.

As Dawson leans to touch my lips with his own I have only one thought:

Dear mama, you would be so proud of the man who swooped in to cherish your daughter and grandchildren. Perhaps you had a hand in sending him to us.

How I hope so…
Oh, how I do hope so.

Printed in Great Britain
by Amazon